KT-372-339

SPECIAL MESSAGE TO READERS

This book is published under the auspices of

THE ULVERSCROFT FOUNDATION

(registered charity No. 264873 UK)

Established in 1972 to provide funds for research, diagnosis and treatment of eye diseases. Examples of contributions made are: —

A Children's Assessment Unit at Moorfield's Hospital, London.

•

Twin operating theatres at the Western Ophthalmic Hospital, London.

•

A Chair of Ophthalmology at the Royal Australian College of Ophthalmologists.

•

The Ulverscroft Children's Eye Unit at the Great Ormond Street Hospital For Sick Children, London.

You can help further the work of the Foundation by making a donation or leaving a legacy. Every contribution, no matter how small, is received with gratitude. Please write for details to:

THE ULVERSCROFT FOUNDATION,
The Green, Bradgate Road, Anstey,
Leicester LE7 7FU, England.
Telephone: (0116) 236 4325

In Australia write to:

THE ULVERSCROFT FOUNDATION,
c/o The Royal Australian College of Ophthalmologists,
27, Commonwealth Street, Sydney,
N.S.W. 2010.

Jeffrey Archer was born in 1940 and educated at Wellington School, Somerset and Brasenose College, Oxford. He represented Great Britain in the 100 metres in the early sixties, and entered the House of Commons when he won the by-election at Louth in 1969. He wrote his first novel, *Not a Penny More, Not a Penny Less*, in 1974. From September 1985 to October 1986 he was Deputy Chairman of the Conservative Party, and he was created a Life Peer in the Queen's Birthday Honours of 1992. He lives in London and Cambridge with his wife and two sons.

THE COLLECTED SHORT STORIES
Volume II

These short stories — drawn from the three volumes: A QUIVER FULL OF ARROWS, A TWIST IN THE TALE and TWELVE RED HERRINGS — show Jeffrey Archer at the peak of his form. His mastery of characterisation and suspense, combined with his great gift for the unexpected plot twist, provides a feast of entertainment for readers old and new.

Books by Jeffrey Archer
Published by The House of Ulverscroft:

NOT A PENNY MORE,
NOT A PENNY LESS
KANE AND ABEL
THE PRODIGAL DAUGHTER
AS THE CROW FLIES
HONOUR AMONG THIEVES
TWELVE RED HERRINGS
THE COLLECTED SHORT STORIES
VOLUME I

JEFFREY ARCHER

THE COLLECTED SHORT STORIES

Volume II

Complete and Unabridged

CHARNWOOD
Leicester

First published in Great Britain in 1997 by
HarperCollins Publishers
London

First Charnwood Edition
published 2002
by arrangement with
HarperCollins Publishers Limited
London

British Library CIP Data

Archer, Jeffrey, *1940 –*
The collected short stories.—Large print ed.—
Vol. 2
Charnwood library series
1. Large type books
I. Title
823.9′14 [F]

ISBN 0–7089–9282–X

Published by
F. A. Thorpe (Publishing)
Anstey, Leicestershire

Set by Words & Graphics Ltd.
Anstey, Leicestershire
Printed and bound in Great Britain by
T. J. International Ltd., Padstow, Cornwall

This book is printed on acid-free paper

To John and Norma

Contents

Colonel Bullfrog

There is one Cathedral in England that has never found it necessary to launch a national appeal.

When the Colonel woke he found himself tied to a stake where the ambush had taken place. He could feel a numb sensation in his leg. The last thing he could recall was the bayonet entering his thigh. All he was aware of now were ants crawling up the leg on an endless march towards the wound.

It would have been better to have remained unconscious, he decided.

Then someone undid the knots and he collapsed head first into the mud. It would be better still to be dead, he concluded. The Colonel somehow got to his knees and crawled over to the stake next to him. Tied to it was a corporal who must have been dead for several hours. Ants were crawling into his mouth. The Colonel tore off a strip from the man's shirt, washed it in a large puddle nearby and cleaned the wound in his leg as best he could before binding it tightly.

That was February 17th, 1943, a date that would be etched on the Colonel's memory for the rest of his life.

That same morning the Japanese received orders that the newly captured Allied prisoners were to be moved at dawn. Many were to die on the march and even more had perished before the trek began. Colonel Richard Moore was determined not to be counted among them.

Twenty-nine days later, one hundred and seventeen of the original seven hundred and thirty-two Allied troops reached Tonchan. Any man whose travels had previously not taken him beyond Rome could hardly have been prepared for such an experience as Tonchan. This heavily guarded prisoner-of-war camp, some three hundred miles north of Singapore and hidden in the deepest equatorial jungle, offered no possibility of freedom. Anyone who contemplated escape could not hope to survive in the jungle for more than a few days, while those who remained discovered the odds were not a lot shorter.

When the Colonel first arrived, Major Sakata, the camp commandant, informed him that he was the senior ranking officer and would therefore be held responsible for the welfare of all Allied troops.

Colonel Moore had stared down at the Japanese officer. Sakata must have been a foot shorter than himself but after that twenty-eight-day march the British soldier couldn't have weighed much more than the diminutive Major.

Moore's first act on leaving the commandant's office was to call together all the Allied officers. He discovered there was a good cross-section from Britain, Australia, New Zealand and America but few could have been described as fit. Men were dying daily from malaria, dysentery and malnutrition. He was suddenly aware what the expression 'dying like flies' meant.

The Colonel learned from his staff officers that for the previous two years of the camp's existence they had been ordered to build bamboo huts for the Japanese officers. These had had to be completed before they had been allowed to start on a hospital for their own men and only recently huts for themselves. Many prisoners had died during those two years, not from illness but from the atrocities some Japanese perpetrated on a daily basis. Major Sakata, known because of his skinny arms as 'Chopsticks', was, however, not considered to be the villain. His second-in-command, Lieutenant Takasaki (the Undertaker), and Sergeant Ayut (the Pig) were of a different mould and to be avoided at all cost, his men warned him.

It took the Colonel only a few days to discover why.

He decided his first task was to try to raise the battered morale of his troops. As there was no padre among those officers who had been captured he began each day by conducting a short service of prayer. Once the service was over the men would start work on the railway that ran alongside the camp. Each arduous day consisted of laying tracks to help Japanese soldiers get to the front more quickly so they could in turn kill and capture more Allied troops. Any prisoner suspected of undermining this work was found guilty of sabotage and put to death without trial. Lieutenant Takasaki considered taking an unscheduled five-minute break to be sabotage.

At lunch prisoners were allowed twenty minutes off to share a bowl of rice — usually with maggots — and, if they were lucky, a mug of water. Although the men returned to the camp each night exhausted, the Colonel still set about organising squads to be responsible for the cleanliness of their huts and the state of the latrines.

After only a few months, the Colonel was able to organise a football match between the British and the Americans, and following its success even set up a camp league. But he was even more delighted when the men turned up for karate lessons under Sergeant Hawke, a thick-set Australian, who had a Black Belt and for good measure also played the mouth organ. The tiny instrument had survived the march through the jungle but everyone assumed it would be discovered before long and confiscated.

Each day Moore renewed his determination not to allow the Japanese to believe for one moment that the Allies were beaten — despite the fact that while he was at Tonchan he lost another twenty pounds in weight, and at least one man under his command every day.

To the Colonel's surprise the camp commandant, despite the Japanese national belief that any soldier who allowed himself to be captured ought to be treated as a deserter, did not place too many unnecessary obstacles in his path.

'You are like the British Bullfrog,' Major Sakata suggested one evening as he watched the Colonel carving cricket bails out of bamboo. It was one of the rare occasions when the Colonel managed a smile.

His real problems continued to come from Lieutenant Takasaki and his henchmen, who considered captured Allied prisoners fit only to be considered as traitors. Takasaki was always careful how he treated the Colonel personally, but felt no such reservations when dealing with the other ranks, with the result that Allied soldiers often ended up with their meagre rations confiscated, a rifle butt in the stomach, or even left bound to a tree for days on end.

Whenever the Colonel made an official complaint to the commandant, Major Sakata listened sympathetically and even made an effort to weed out the main offenders. Moore's happiest moment at Tonchan was to witness the Undertaker and the Pig boarding the train for the front line. No one attempted to sabotage that journey. The commandant replaced them with Sergeant Akida and Corporal Sushi, known by the prisoners almost affectionately as 'Sweet and Sour Pork'. However, the Japanese High Command sent a new Number Two to the camp, a Lieutenant Osawa, who quickly became known as 'The Devil' since he perpetrated atrocities that made the Undertaker and the Pig look like church fête organisers.

As the months passed the Colonel and the commandant's mutual respect grew. Sakata even confided to his English prisoner that he had requested that he be sent to the front line and join the real war. 'And if,' the Major added, 'the High Command grants my request, there will be only two NCOs I would want to accompany me.'

Colonel Moore knew the Major had Sweet and Sour Pork in mind, and was fearful what might become of his men if the only three Japanese he could work with were posted back to active duties to leave Lieutenant Osawa in command of the camp.

⋆ ⋆ ⋆

Colonel Moore realised that something quite extraordinary must have taken place for Major Sakata to come to his hut, because he had never done so before. The Colonel put his bowl of rice back down on the table and asked the three Allied officers who were sharing breakfast with him to wait outside.

The Major stood to attention and saluted.

The Colonel pushed himself to his full six feet, returned the salute and stared down into Sakata's eyes.

'The war is over,' said the Japanese officer. For a brief moment Moore feared the worst. 'Japan has surrendered unconditionally. You, sir,' Sakata said quietly, 'are now in command of the camp.'

The Colonel immediately ordered all Japanese officers to be placed under arrest in the commandant's quarters. While his orders were being carried out he personally went in search of The Devil. Moore marched across the parade ground and headed towards the officers' quarters. He located the second-in-command's hut, walked up the steps and threw open Osawa's door. The sight that met the new commandant's eyes was one he would never forget. The Colonel had read of ceremonial harakiri without any real idea of what the final act consisted. Lieutenant Osawa must have cut himself a hundred times before he eventually died. The blood, the stench and the sight of the mutilated body would have caused a Gurkha to be sick. Only the head was there to confirm that the remains had once belonged to a human being.

The Colonel ordered Osawa to be buried outside the gates of the camp.

⋆ ⋆ ⋆

When the surrender of Japan was finally signed on board the USS *Missouri* in Tokyo Bay, all at Tonchan PoW camp listened to the ceremony on the single camp radio. Colonel Moore then called a full parade on the camp square. For the first time in two and a half years he wore his dress uniform which made him look like a pierrot who had turned up at a formal party. He accepted the Japanese flag of surrender from Major Sakata on behalf of the Allies, then made the defeated enemy raise the American and British flags to the sound of both national anthems played in turn by Sergeant Hawke on his mouth organ.

The Colonel then held a short service of thanksgiving which he conducted in the presence of all the Allied and Japanese soldiers.

⋆ ⋆ ⋆

Once command had changed hands Colonel Moore waited as week followed pointless week for news that he would be sent home. Many of his men had been given their orders to start the ten-thousand-mile journey back to England via Bangkok and Calcutta, but no such orders came for the Colonel and he waited in vain to be sent his repatriation papers.

Then, in January 1946, a smartly dressed young Guards officer arrived at the camp with orders to see the Colonel. He was conducted to the commandant's office and saluted before shaking hands. Richard Moore stared at the young captain who, from his healthy complexion, had obviously arrived in the Far East long after the Japanese had surrendered. The captain handed over a letter to the Colonel.

'Home at last,' said the older man breezily, as he ripped open the envelope, only to discover that it would be years before he could hope to exchange the paddy fields of Tonchan for the green fields of Lincolnshire.

The letter requested that the Colonel travel to Tokyo and represent Britain on the forthcoming war tribunal which was to be conducted in the Japanese capital. Captain Ross of the Coldstream Guards would take over his command at Tonchan.

* * *

The tribunal was to consist of twelve officers under the chairmanship of General Matthew Tomkins. Moore was to be the sole British representative and was to report directly to the General, 'as soon as you find it convenient'. Further details would be supplied to him on his arrival in Tokyo. The letter ended: 'If for any reason you should require my help in your deliberations, do not hesitate to contact me personally.' There followed the signature of Clement Attlee.

Staff officers are not in the habit of disobeying Prime Ministers, so the Colonel resigned himself to a prolonged stay in Japan.

It took several months to set up the tribunal and during that time Colonel Moore continued supervising the return of British troops to their homeland. The paperwork was endless and some of the men under his command were so frail that he found it necessary to build them up spiritually as well as physically before he could put them on boats to their various destinations. Some died long after the declaration of surrender had been ratified.

During this period of waiting, Colonel Moore used Major Sakata and the two NCOs in whom he had placed so much trust, Sergeant Akida and Corporal Sushi, as his liaison officers. This sudden change of command did not affect the relationship between the two senior officers, although Sakata admitted to the Colonel that he wished he had been killed in the defence of his country and not left to witness its humiliations. The Colonel found the Japanese remained well-disciplined while they waited to learn their fate, and most of them assumed death was the natural consequence of defeat.

* * *

The war tribunal held its first plenary session in Tokyo on April 19th, 1946. General Tomkins took over the fifth floor of the old Imperial Courthouse in the Ginza quarter of Tokyo — one of the few buildings that had survived the war intact. Tomkins, a squat, short-tempered man who was described by his own staff officer as a 'penpusher from the Pentagon', arrived in Tokyo only a week before he began his first deliberations. The only rat-a-tat-tat this General had ever heard, the staff officer freely admitted to Colonel Moore, had come from the typewriter in his secretary's office. However, when it came to those on trial the General was in no doubt as to where the guilt lay and how the guilty should be punished.

'Hang every one of the little slit-eyed, yellow bastards,' turned out to be one of Tomkins's favourite expressions.

Seated round a table in an old courtroom, the twelve-man tribunal conducted their deliberations. It was clear from the opening session that the General had no intention of considering 'extenuating circumstances', 'past record' or 'humanitarian grounds'. As the Colonel listened to Tomkins's views he began to fear for the lives of any innocent member of the armed forces who was brought in front of the General.

The Colonel quickly identified four Americans from the tribunal who, like himself, did not always concur with the General's sweeping judgements. Two were lawyers and the other two had been fighting soldiers recently involved in combat duty. The five men began to work together to counteract the General's most prejudiced decisions. During the following weeks they were able to persuade one or two others around the table to commute the sentences of hanging to life imprisonment for several Japanese who had been condemned for crimes they could not possibly have committed.

As each such case was debated, General Tomkins left the five men in no doubt as to his contempt for their views. 'Goddam Nip sympathisers,' he often suggested, and not always under his breath. As the General still held sway over the twelve-man tribunal, the Colonel's successes turned out to be few in number.

When the time came to determine the fate of those who had been in command of the PoW camp at Tonchan the General demanded mass hanging for every Japanese officer involved without even the pretence of a proper trial. He showed no surprise when the usual five tribunal members raised their voices in protest. Colonel Moore spoke eloquently of having been a prisoner at Tonchan and petitioned in the defence of Major Sakata, Sergeant Akida and Corporal Sushi. He attempted to explain why hanging them would in its own way be as barbaric as any atrocity carried out by the Japanese. He insisted their sentence should be commuted to life imprisonment. The General yawned throughout the Colonel's remarks and, once Moore had completed his case, made no attempt to justify his position but simply called for a vote. To the General's surprise, the result was six-all; an American lawyer who previously had sided with the General raised his hand to join the Colonel's five. Without hesitation the General threw his casting vote in favour of the gallows. Tomkins leered down the table at Moore and said, 'Time for lunch, I think, gentlemen. I don't know about you but I'm famished. And no one can say that this time we didn't give the little yellow bastards a fair hearing.'

Colonel Moore rose from his place and without offering an opinion left the room.

He ran down the steps of the courthouse and instructed his driver to take him to British HQ in the centre of the city as quickly as possible. The short journey took them some time because of the mêlée of people that were always thronging the streets night and day. Once the Colonel arrived at his office he asked his secretary to place a call through to England. While she was carrying out his order Moore went to his green cabinet and thumbed through several files until he reached the one marked 'Personal'. He opened it and fished out the letter. He wanted to be certain that he had remembered the sentence accurately . . .

'If for any reason you should require my help in your deliberations, do not hesitate to contact me personally.'

'He's coming to the phone, sir,' the secretary said nervously. The Colonel walked over to the phone and waited. He found himself standing to attention when he heard the gentle, cultivated voice ask, 'Is that you, Colonel?' It took Richard

Moore less than ten minutes to explain the problem he faced and obtain the authority he needed.

Immediately he had completed his conversation he returned to the tribunal headquarters. He marched straight back into the conference room just as General Tomkins was settling down in his chair to start the afternoon proceedings.

The Colonel was the first to rise from his place when the General declared the tribunal to be in session. 'I wonder if I might be allowed to open with a statement?' he requested.

'Be my guest,' said Tomkins. 'But make it brief. We've got a lot more of these Japs to get through yet.'

Colonel Moore looked around the table at the other eleven men.

'Gentlemen,' he began. 'I hereby resign my position as the British representative on this commission.'

General Tomkins was unable to stifle a smile.

'I do it,' the Colonel continued, 'reluctantly, but with the backing of my Prime Minister, to whom I spoke only a few moments ago.' At this piece of information Tomkins's smile was replaced by a frown. 'I shall be returning to England in order to make a full report to Mr Attlee and the British Cabinet on the manner in which this tribunal is being conducted.'

'Now look here, sonny,' began the General. 'You can't — '

'I can, sir, and I will. Unlike you, I am unwilling to have the blood of innocent soldiers on my hands for the rest of my life.'

'Now look here, sonny,' the General repeated. 'Let's at least talk this through before you do anything you might regret.'

There was no break for the rest of that day, and by late afternoon Major Sakata, Sergeant Akida and Corporal Sushi had had their sentences commuted to life imprisonment.

Within a month, General Tomkins had been recalled by the Pentagon to be replaced by a distinguished American marine who had been decorated in combat during the First World War.

In the weeks that followed the new appointment the death sentences of two hundred and twenty-nine Japanese prisoners of war were commuted.

Colonel Moore returned to Lincolnshire on November 11th, 1948, having had enough of the realities of war and the hypocrisies of peace.

* * *

Just under two years later Richard Moore took holy orders and became a parish priest in the sleepy hamlet of Weddlebeach, in Suffolk. He enjoyed his calling and although he rarely mentioned his wartime experiences to his parishioners he often thought of his days in Japan.

'Blessed are the peacemakers for they shall . . . ' the vicar began his sermon from the pulpit one Palm Sunday morning in the early 1960s, but he failed to complete the sentence.

His parishioners looked up anxiously only to

see that a broad smile had spread across the vicar's face as he gazed down at someone seated in the third row.

The man he was staring at bowed his head in embarrassment and the vicar quickly continued with his sermon.

When the service was over Richard Moore waited by the west door to be sure his eyes had not deceived him. When they met face to face for the first time in fifteen years both men bowed and then shook hands.

The priest was delighted to learn over lunch that day back at the vicarage that Chopsticks Sakata had been released from prison after only five years, following the Allies' agreement with the newly installed Japanese government to release all prisoners who had not committed capital crimes. When the Colonel enquired after 'Sweet and Sour Pork' the Major admitted that he had lost touch with Sergeant Akida (Sweet) but that Corporal Sushi (Sour) and he were working for the same electronics company. 'And whenever we meet,' he assured the priest, 'we talk of the honourable man who saved our lives, 'the British Bullfrog'.'

* * *

Over the years, the priest and his Japanese friend progressed in their chosen professions and regularly corresponded with each other. In 1971 Ari Sakata was put in charge of a large electronics factory in Osaka while eighteen months later Richard Moore became the Very

Revd Richard Moore, Dean of Lincoln Cathedral.

'I read in *The Times* that your cathedral is appealing for a new roof,' wrote Sakata from his homeland in 1975.

'Nothing unusual about that,' the Dean explained in his letter of reply. 'There isn't a cathedral in England that doesn't suffer from dry rot or bomb damage. The former I fear is terminal; the latter at least has the chance of a cure.'

A few weeks later the Dean received a cheque for ten thousand pounds from a not-unknown Japanese electronics company.

When in 1979 the Very Revd Richard Moore was appointed to the bishopric of Taunton, the new managing director of the largest electronics company in Japan flew over to attend his enthronement.

'I see you have another roof problem,' commented Ari Sakata as he gazed up at the scaffolding surrounding the pulpit. 'How much will it cost this time?'

'At least twenty-five thousand pounds a year,' replied the Bishop without thought. 'Just to make sure the roof doesn't fall in on the congregation during my sterner sermons.' He sighed as he passed the evidence of reconstruction all around him. 'As soon as I've settled into my new job I intend to launch a proper appeal to ensure my successor doesn't have to worry about the roof ever again.'

The managing director nodded his understanding. A week later a cheque for twenty-five thousand pounds arrived on the churchman's desk.

The Bishop tried hard to express his grateful thanks. He knew he must never allow Chopsticks to feel that by his generosity he might have done the wrong thing as this would only insult his friend and undoubtedly end their relationship. Rewrite after rewrite was drafted to ensure that the final version of the long hand-written letter would have passed muster with the Foreign Office mandarin in charge of the Japanese desk. Finally the letter was posted.

As the years passed Richard Moore became fearful of writing to his old friend more than once a year as each letter elicited an even larger cheque. And, when towards the end of 1986 he did write, he made no reference to the Dean and Chapter's decision to designate 1988 as the cathedral's appeal year. Nor did he mention his own failing health, lest the old Japanese gentleman should feel in some way responsible, as his doctor had warned him that he could never expect to recover fully from those experiences at Tonchan.

The Bishop set about forming his appeal committee in January 1987. The Prince of Wales became the patron and the Lord Lieutenant of the county its chairman. In his opening address to the members of the appeal committee the Bishop instructed them that it was their duty to raise not less than three million pounds during 1988. Some apprehensive looks appeared on the faces around the table.

On August 11th, 1987, the Bishop of Taunton was umpiring a village cricket match when he suddenly collapsed from a heart attack. 'See that the appeal brochures are printed in time for the next meeting,' were his final words to the captain of the local team.

Bishop Moore's memorial service was held in Taunton Cathedral and conducted by the Archbishop of Canterbury. Not a seat could be found in the cathedral that day, and so many crowded into every pew that the west door was left open. Those who arrived late had to listen to the Archbishop's address relayed over loudspeakers placed around the market square.

Casual onlookers must have been puzzled by the presence of several elderly Japanese gentlemen dotted around the congregation.

When the service came to an end the Archbishop held a private meeting in the vestry of the cathedral with the chairman of the largest electronics company in the world.

'You must be Mr Sakata,' said the Archbishop, warmly shaking the hand of a man who stepped forward from the small cluster of Japanese who were in attendance. 'Thank you for taking the trouble to write and let me know that you would be coming. I am delighted to meet you at last. The Bishop always spoke of you with great affection and as a close friend — 'Chopsticks', if I remember.'

Mr Sakata bowed low.

'And I also know that he always considered himself in your personal debt for such generosity over so many years.'

'No, no, not me,' replied the former Major. 'I, like my dear friend the late Bishop, am representative of higher authority.'

The Archbishop looked puzzled.

'You see, sir,' continued Mr Sakata, 'I am only the chairman of the company. May I have the honour of introducing my President?'

Mr Sakata took a pace backwards to allow an even smaller figure, whom the Archbishop had originally assumed to be part of Mr Sakata's entourage, to step forward.

The President bowed low and, still without speaking, passed an envelope to the Archbishop.

'May I be allowed to open it?' the church leader asked, unaware of the Japanese custom of waiting until the giver has departed.

The little man bowed again.

The Archbishop slit open the envelope and removed a cheque for three million pounds.

'The late Bishop must have been a very close friend,' was all he could think of saying.

'No, sir,' the President replied. 'I did not have that privilege.'

'Then he must have done something incredible to be deserving of such a munificent gesture.'

'He performed an act of honour over forty years ago and now I try inadequately to repay it.'

'Then he would surely have remembered you,' said the Archbishop.

'Is possible he would remember me but if so only as the sour half of 'Sweet and Sour Pork'.'

* * *

There is one cathedral in England that has never found it necessary to launch a national appeal.

Clean Sweep Ignatius

Few showed much interest when Ignatius Agarbi was appointed Nigeria's Minister of Finance. After all, the cynics pointed out, he was the seventeenth person to hold the office in seventeen years.

In Ignatius's first major policy statement to Parliament he promised to end graft and corruption in public life and warned the electorate that no one holding an official position could feel safe unless he led a blameless life. He ended his maiden speech with the words, 'I intend to clear out Nigeria's Augean stables.'

Such was the impact of the minister's speech that it failed to get a mention in the Lagos *Daily Times*. Perhaps the editor considered that, since the paper had covered the speeches of the previous sixteen ministers *in extenso*, his readers might feel they had heard it all before.

Ignatius, however, was not disheartened by the lack of confidence shown in him, and set about his new task with vigour and determination. Within days of his appointment he had caused a minor official at the Ministry of Trade to be jailed for falsifying documents relating to the import of grain. The next to feel the bristles of Ignatius's new broom was a leading Lebanese financier, who was deported without trial for breach of the exchange control regulations. A month later came an event which even Ignatius considered a personal coup: the arrest of the Inspector General of Police for accepting bribes — a perk the citizens of Lagos had in the past considered went with the job. When four months later the Police Chief was sentenced to eighteen months in jail, the new Finance Minister finally made the front page of the Lagos *Daily Times*. A leader on the centre page dubbed him 'Clean Sweep Ignatius', the new broom every guilty man feared. Ignatius's reputation as Mr Clean continued to grow as arrest followed arrest, and unfounded rumours began circulating in the capital that even General Otobi, the Head of State, was under investigation by his own Finance Minister.

Ignatius alone now checked, vetted and authorised all foreign contracts worth over one hundred million dollars. And although every decision he made was meticulously scrutinised by his enemies, not a breath of scandal ever became associated with his name.

When Ignatius began his second year of office as Minister of Finance even the cynics began to acknowledge his achievements. It was about this time that General Otobi felt confident enough to call him in for an unscheduled consultation.

The Head of State welcomed the Minister to Dodan Barracks and ushered him to a comfortable chair in his study overlooking the parade ground.

'Ignatius, I have just finished going over the latest budget report, and I am alarmed by your conclusion that the Exchequer is still losing millions of dollars each year in bribes paid to go-betweens by foreign companies. Have you any idea into whose pockets this money is falling? That's what I want to know.'

Ignatius sat bolt upright, his eyes never leaving the Head of State.

'I suspect a great percentage of the money is ending up in private Swiss bank accounts, but I am at present unable to prove it.'

'Then I will give you whatever added authority you require to do so,' said General Otobi. 'You can use any means you consider necessary to ferret out these villains. Start by investigating every member of my Cabinet, past and present. And show no fear or favour in your endeavours, no matter what their rank or connections.'

'For such a task to have any chance of success I would need a special letter of authority signed by you, General . . . '

'Then it will be on your desk by six o'clock this evening,' said the Head of State.

'And the rank of Ambassador Plenipotentiary whenever I travel abroad.'

'Granted.'

'Thank you,' said Ignatius, rising from his chair on the assumption that the audience was over.

'You may also need this,' said the General as they walked towards the door. The Head of State handed Ignatius a small automatic pistol. 'Because I suspect by now that you have almost as many enemies as I.'

Ignatius took the pistol from the soldier awkwardly, put it in his pocket and mumbled his thanks.

Without another word passing between the two men, Ignatius left his leader and was driven back to his Ministry.

Without the knowledge of the Governor of the Central Bank of Nigeria, and unhindered by any senior civil servants, Ignatius enthusiastically set about his new task. He researched alone at night, and by day discussed his findings with no one. Three months later he was ready to pounce.

The Minister selected the month of August to make an unscheduled visit abroad, as it was the time when most Nigerians went on holiday, and his absence would therefore not be worthy of comment.

He asked his Permanent Secretary to book him, his wife and their two children on a flight to Orlando, and to be certain that the tickets were charged to his personal account.

On their arrival in Florida, the family checked into the local Marriott Hotel. Ignatius then informed his wife, without warning or explanation, that he would be spending a few days in New York on business before rejoining them for the rest of the holiday. The following morning he left his family to the mysteries of Disneyworld while he took a flight to New York. It was a short taxi ride from LaGuardia to Kennedy, where, after a change of clothes and the purchase of a return tourist ticket for cash, he boarded a Swissair flight for Geneva unobserved.

Once he had arrived, Ignatius booked into an inconspicuous hotel, retired to bed and slept soundly for eight hours. Over breakfast the following morning he studied the list of banks he had so carefully drawn up after completing his research in Nigeria: each name was written out boldly in his own hand. Ignatius decided to start with Gerber et Cie, whose building, he observed from the hotel bedroom, took up half the Avenue de Parchine. He checked the telephone number with the concierge before placing a call. The chairman agreed to see him at twelve o'clock.

Carrying only a battered briefcase, Ignatius arrived at the bank a few minutes before the appointed hour — an unusual occurrence for a Nigerian, thought the young man dressed in a smart grey suit, white shirt and grey silk tie who was waiting in the marble hall to greet him. He bowed to the Minister, introducing himself as the chairman's personal assistant, and explained that he would accompany Ignatius to the chairman's office. The young executive led the Minister to a waiting lift and neither man uttered another word until they had reached the eleventh floor. A gentle tap on the chairman's door elicited '*Entrez*,' which the young man obeyed.

'The Nigerian Minister of Finance, sir.'

The chairman rose from behind his desk and stepped forward to greet his guest. Ignatius could not help noticing that he too wore a grey suit, white shirt and grey silk tie.

'Good morning, Minister,' the chairman said. 'Won't you have a seat?' He ushered Ignatius towards a low glass table surrounded by comfortable chairs on the far side of the room. 'I have ordered coffee for both of us, if that is acceptable.'

Ignatius nodded, placed the battered briefcase

on the floor by the side of his chair and stared out of the large plate-glass window. He made some small-talk about the splendid view of the magnificent fountain while a girl served all three men with coffee.

Once the young woman had left the room, Ignatius got down to business.

'My Head of State has asked me to visit your bank with a rather unusual request,' he began. Not a flicker of surprise appeared on the face of the chairman or his young assistant. 'He has honoured me with the task of discovering which Nigerian citizens hold numbered accounts with your bank.'

On learning this piece of information only the chairman's lips moved. 'I am not at liberty to disclose — '

'Allow me to put my case,' said the Minister, raising a white palm. 'First, let me assure you that I come with the absolute authority of my government.' Without another word, Ignatius extracted an envelope from his inside pocket with a flourish. He handed it to the chairman, who removed the letter inside and read it slowly.

Once he had finished reading, the banker cleared his throat. 'This document, I fear, sir, carries no validity in my country.' He replaced it in the envelope and handed it back to Ignatius. 'I am, of course,' continued the chairman, 'not for one moment doubting that you have the full backing of your Head of State, both as a Minister and an Ambassador, but that does not change the bank's rule of confidentiality in such matters. There are no circumstances in which we would release the names of any of our account holders without their authority. I'm sorry to be of so little help, but those are, and will always remain, the bank rules.' The chairman rose to his feet, as he considered the meeting was now at an end; but he had not bargained for Clean Sweep Ignatius.

'My Head of State,' said Ignatius, softening his tone perceptibly, 'has authorised me to approach your bank to act as the intermediary for all future transactions between my country and Switzerland.'

'We are flattered by your confidence in us, Minister,' replied the chairman, who remained standing. 'However, I feel sure that you will understand that it cannot alter our attitude to our customers' confidentiality.'

Ignatius remained unperturbed.

'Then I am sorry to inform you, Mr Gerber, that our Ambassador in Geneva will be instructed to send an official communiqué to the Swiss Foreign Office about the lack of co-operation your bank has shown concerning requests for information about our nationals.' He waited for his words to sink in. 'You could avoid such embarrassment, of course, by simply letting me know the names of my countrymen who hold accounts with Gerber et Cie and the amounts involved. I can assure you we would not reveal the source of our information.'

'You are most welcome to lodge such a communiqué, sir, and I feel sure that our Minister will explain to your Ambassador in the most courteous of diplomatic language that the

Foreign Ministry does not have the authority under Swiss law to demand such disclosures.'

'If that is the case, I shall instruct my own Ministry of Trade to halt all future dealings in Nigeria with any Swiss nationals until these names are revealed.'

'That is your privilege, Minister,' replied the chairman, unmoved.

'And we may also have to reconsider every contract currently being negotiated by your countrymen in Nigeria. And in addition, I shall personally see to it that no penalty clauses are honoured.'

'Would you not consider such action a little precipitate?'

'Let me assure you, Mr Gerber, that I would not lose one moment of sleep over such a decision,' said Ignatius. 'Even if my efforts to discover those names were to bring your country to its knees I would not be moved.'

'So be it, Minister,' replied the chairman. 'However, it still does not alter the policy or the attitude of this bank to confidentiality.'

'If that remains the case, sir, this very day I shall give instructions to our Ambassador to close our Embassy in Geneva, and I shall declare your Ambassador in Lagos *persona non grata*.'

For the first time the chairman raised his eyebrows.

'Furthermore,' continued Ignatius, 'I will hold a press conference in London which will leave the world's media in no doubt of my Head of State's displeasure with the conduct of this bank. After such publicity, I feel confident you will find that many of your customers would prefer to close their accounts, while others who have in the past considered you a safe haven may find it necessary to look elsewhere.'

The Minister waited, but still the chairman did not respond.

'Then you leave me no choice,' said Ignatius, rising from his seat.

The chairman stretched out his arm, assuming that at last the Minister was leaving, only to watch with horror as Ignatius placed a hand in his jacket pocket and removed a small pistol. The two Swiss bankers froze as the Nigerian Minister of Finance stepped forward and pressed the muzzle against the chairman's temple.

'I need those names, Mr Gerber, and by now you must realise I will stop at nothing. If you don't supply them immediately, I'm going to blow your brains out. Do you understand?'

The chairman gave a slight nod, beads of sweat appearing on his forehead. 'And he will be next,' said Ignatius, gesturing towards the young assistant, who stood speechless and paralysed a few paces away.

'Get me the names of every Nigerian who holds an account in this bank,' Ignatius said quietly, looking towards the young man, 'or I'll blow your chairman's brains all over his soft pile carpet. Immediately, do you hear me?' he added sharply.

The young man looked towards the chairman, who was now trembling, but who said quite clearly, '*Non, Pierre, jamais*.'

'*D'accord*,' replied the assistant in a whisper.

'You can't say I didn't give you every chance.' Ignatius pulled back the hammer. The sweat was now pouring down the chairman's face, and the young man had to turn his eyes away as he waited in terror for the pistol shot.

'Excellent,' said Ignatius, as he removed the gun from the chairman's head and returned to his seat. Both the bankers were still trembling and quite unable to speak.

The Minister picked up the battered briefcase by the side of his chair and placed it on the glass table in front of him. He pressed back the clasps and the lid flicked up.

The two bankers stared down at the neatly packed rows of hundred-dollar bills. Every inch of the briefcase had been taken up. The chairman quickly estimated that it probably amounted to around five million dollars.

'I wonder, sir,' said Ignatius, 'how I go about opening an account with your bank?'

One-Night Stand

The two men had first met at the age of five when they were placed side by side at school, for no more compelling reason than that their names, Thompson and Townsend, came one after the other on the class register. They soon became best friends, a tie which at that age is more binding than any marriage. After passing their eleven-plus examination they proceeded to the local grammar school with no Timpsons, Tooleys or Tomlinsons to divide them and, having completed seven years in that academic institution, reached an age when one either has to go to work or to university. They opted for the latter on the grounds that work should be put off until the last possible moment. Happily, they both possessed enough brains and native wit to earn themselves places at Durham University to read English.

Undergraduate life turned out to be as sociable as primary school. They both enjoyed English, tennis, cricket, good food and girls. Luckily, in the last of these predilections they differed only on points of detail. Michael, who was six-foot-two, willowy with dark curly hair, preferred tall, bosomy blondes with blue eyes and long legs. Adrian, a stocky man of five-foot-ten, with straight, sandy hair, always fell for small, slim, dark-haired, dark-eyed girls. So whenever Adrian came across a girl that Michael took an interest in or vice versa, whether she was an undergraduate or barmaid, either one would happily exaggerate his friend's virtues. Thus they spent three idyllic years in unison at Durham, gaining considerably more than a Bachelor of Arts degree. As neither of them had impressed the examiners enough to waste a further two years expounding their theories for a Ph.D they could no longer avoid the real world.

Twin Dick Whittingtons, they set off for London, where Michael joined the BBC as a trainee while Adrian was signed up by Benton & Bowles, the international advertising agency, as an account assistant. They acquired a small flat in the Earls Court Road which they painted orange and brown, and proceeded to live the life of two young blades, for that is undoubtedly how they saw themselves.

Both men spent a further five years in this blissful bachelor state until each fell for a girl who fulfilled his particular requirements. They were married within weeks of each other: Michael to a tall, blue-eyed blonde whom he met while playing tennis at the Hurlingham Club, Adrian to a slim, dark-eyed, dark-haired executive in charge of the Kellogg's Cornflakes account. Each officiated as the other's best man and each proceeded to sire three children at yearly intervals, and in that again they differed, but as before only on points of detail, Michael having two sons and a daughter, Adrian two daughters and a son. Each became godfather to the other's first-born son.

Marriage hardly separated them in anything as

they continued to follow much of their old routine, playing cricket together at weekends in the summer and football in the winter, not to mention regular luncheons during the week.

After the celebration of his tenth wedding anniversary, Michael, now a senior producer with Thames Television, admitted rather coyly to Adrian that he had had his first affair: he had been unable to resist a tall, well-built blonde from the typing pool who was offering more than shorthand at seventy words a minute. Only a few weeks later, Adrian, now a senior account manager with Pearl and Dean, also went under, selecting a journalist from Fleet Street who was seeking some inside information on one of the companies he represented. She became a tax-deductible item. After that, the two men quickly fell back into their old routine. Any help they could give each other was provided unstintingly, creating no conflict of interests because of their different tastes. Their married lives were not suffering — or so they convinced each other — and at thirty-five, having come through the swinging sixties unscathed, they began to make the most of the seventies.

Early in that decade, Thames Television decided to send Michael off to America to edit an ABC film about living in New York, for consumption by British viewers. Adrian, who had always wanted to see the eastern seaboard, did not find it hard to arrange a trip at the same time as he claimed it was necessary for him to carry out some more than usually spurious research for an Anglo-American tobacco company. The two men enjoyed a lively week together in New York, the highlight of which was a party held by ABC on the final evening to view the edited edition of Michael's film on New York, *An Englishman's View of the Big Apple*.

When Michael and Adrian arrived at the ABC studios they found the party was already well under way, and they entered the room together, looking forward to a few drinks and an early night before their journey back to England the next day.

They spotted her at exactly the same moment.

She was of medium height and build, with soft green eyes and auburn hair — a striking combination of both men's fantasies. Without another thought each knew exactly where he desired to end up that particular night and, two minds with but a single idea, they advanced purposefully upon her.

'Hello, my name is Michael Thompson.'

'Hello,' she replied. 'I'm Debbie Kendall.'

'And I'm Adrian Townsend.'

She offered her hand and both tried to grab it. When the party had come to an end, they had, between them, discovered that Debbie Kendall was an ABC floor producer on the evening news spot. She was divorced and had two children who lived with her in New York. But neither of them was any nearer to impressing her, if only because each worked so hard to outdo the other; they both showed off abominably and even squabbled over fetching their new companion her food and drink. In the other's absence they found themselves running down their closest friend in a subtle but damning way.

'Adrian's a nice chap if it wasn't for his drinking,' said Michael.

'Super fellow Michael, such a lovely wife and you should see his three adorable children,' added Adrian.

They both escorted Debbie home and reluctantly left her on the doorstep of her 68th Street apartment. She kissed the two of them perfunctorily on the cheek, thanked them and said goodnight. They walked back to their hotel in silence.

When they reached their room on the nineteenth floor of the Plaza, it was Michael who spoke first.

'I'm sorry,' he said. 'I made a bloody fool of myself.'

'I was every bit as bad,' said Adrian. 'We shouldn't fight over a woman. We never have done in the past.'

'Agreed,' said Michael. 'So why not an honourable compromise?'

'What do you suggest?'

'As we both return to London tomorrow morning, let's agree whichever one of us comes back first . . . '

'Perfect,' said Adrian and they shook hands to seal the bargain, as if they were both back at school playing a cricket match, and had to decide on who should bat first. The deal made, they climbed into their respective beds, and slept soundly.

* * *

Once back in London both men did everything in their power to find an excuse for returning to New York. Neither contacted Debbie Kendall by phone or letter, as it would have broken their gentleman's agreement, but when the weeks grew to be months both became despondent and it seemed that neither was going to be given the opportunity to return. Then Adrian was invited to Los Angeles to address a Media Conference. He remained unbearably smug about the whole trip, confident he would be able to drop into New York on the way to London. It was Michael who discovered that British Airways were offering cheap tickets for wives who accompanied their husbands on a business trip: Adrian was therefore unable to return via New York. Michael breathed a sigh of relief which turned to triumph when he was selected to go to Washington and cover the president's Address to Congress. He suggested to the head of Outside Broadcasts that it would be wise to drop into New York on the way home and strengthen the contacts he had previously made with ABC. The head of Outside Broadcasts agreed, but told Michael he must be back the following day to cover the opening of Parliament.

Adrian phoned up Michael's wife and briefed her on cheap trips to the States when accompanying your husband. 'How kind of you to be so thoughtful Adrian but alas my school never allows time off during term, and in any case,' she added, 'I have a dreadful fear of flying.'

Michael was very understanding about his wife's phobia and went off to book a single ticket.

* * *

Michael flew into Washington on the following Monday and called Debbie Kendall from his hotel room, wondering if she would even remember the two vainglorious Englishmen she had briefly met some months before, and if she did whether she would also recall which one he was. He dialled nervously and listened to the ringing tone. Was she in, was she even in New York? At last a click and a soft voice said hello.

'Hello, Debbie, it's Michael Thompson.'

'Hello, Michael. What a nice surprise. Are you in New York?'

'No, Washington, but I'm thinking of flying up. You wouldn't be free for dinner on Thursday by any chance?'

'Let me just check my diary.'

Michael held his breath as he waited. It seemed like hours.

'Yes, that seems to be fine.'

'Fantastic. Shall I pick you up around eight?'

'Yes, thank you, Michael. I'll look forward to seeing you then.'

Heartened by this early success Michael immediately penned a telegram of commiseration to Adrian on his sad loss. Adrian didn't reply.

Michael took the shuttle up to New York on the Thursday afternoon as soon as he had finished editing the President's speech for the London office. After settling into another hotel room — this time insisting on a double bed just in case Debbie's children were at home — he had a long bath and a slow shave, cutting himself twice and slapping on a little too much aftershave. He rummaged around for his most telling tie, shirt and suit, and after he had finished dressing he studied himself in the mirror, carefully combing his freshly washed hair to make the long thin strands appear casual as well as cover the parts where his hair was beginning to recede. After a final check, he was able to convince himself that he looked less than his thirty-eight years. Michael then took the lift down to the ground floor, and stepping out of the Plaza on to a neon-lit Fifth Avenue he headed jauntily towards 68th Street. En route, he acquired a dozen roses from a little shop at the corner of 65th Street and Madison Avenue and, humming to himself, proceeded confidently. He arrived at the front door of Debbie Kendall's little brownstone at eight-five.

When Debbie opened the door, Michael thought she looked even more beautiful than he had remembered. She was wearing a long blue dress with a frilly white silk collar and cuffs that covered every part of her body from neck to ankles and yet she could not have been more desirable. She wore almost no make-up except a touch of lipstick that Michael already had plans to remove. Her green eyes sparkled.

'Say something,' she said smiling.

'You look quite stunning, Debbie,' was all he

could think of as he handed her the roses.

'How sweet of you,' she replied and invited him in.

Michael followed her into the kitchen where she hammered the long stems and arranged the flowers in a porcelain vase. She then led him into the living room, where she placed the roses on an oval table beside a photograph of two small boys.

'Have we time for a drink?'

'Sure. I've booked a table at Elaine's for eight-thirty.'

'My favourite restaurant,' she said, with a smile that revealed a small dimple on her cheek. Without asking, Debbie poured two whiskies and handed one of them to Michael.

What a good memory she has, he thought, as he nervously kept picking up and putting down his glass, like a teenager on his first date. When Michael had eventually finished his drink, Debbie suggested that they should leave.

'Elaine wouldn't keep a table free for one minute, even if you were Henry Kissinger.'

Michael laughed, and helped her on with her coat. As she unlatched the door, he realised there was no baby-sitter or sound of children. They must be staying with their father, he thought. Once on the street, he hailed a cab and directed the driver to 87th and 2nd. Michael had never been to Elaine's before. The restaurant had been recommended by a friend from ABC who had assured him: 'That joint will give you more than half a chance.'

As they entered the crowded room and waited

by the bar for the maître d', Michael could see it was the type of place that was frequented by the rich and famous and wondered if his pocket could stand the expense and, more importantly, whether such an outlay would turn out to be a worthwhile investment.

A waiter guided them to a small table at the back of the room, where they both had another whisky while they studied the menu. When the waiter returned to take their order, Debbie wanted no first course, just the veal piccate, so Michael ordered the same for himself. She refused the addition of garlic butter. Michael allowed his expectations to rise slightly.

'How's Adrian?' she asked.

'Oh, as well as can be expected,' Michael replied. 'He sends you his love, of course.' He emphasised the word love.

'How kind of him to remember me, and please return mine. What brings you to New York this time, Michael? Another film?'

'No. New York may well have become everybody's second city, but this time I only came to see you.'

'To see me?'

'Yes, I had a tape to edit while I was in Washington, but I always knew I could be through with that by lunch today so I hoped you would be free to spend an evening with me.'

'I'm flattered.'

'You shouldn't be.'

She smiled. The veal arrived.

'Looks good,' said Michael.

'Tastes good, too,' said Debbie. 'When do you fly home?'

'Tomorrow morning, eleven o'clock flight, I'm afraid.'

'Not left yourself time to do much in New York.'

'I only came up to see you,' Michael repeated. Debbie continued eating her veal. 'Why would any man want to divorce you, Debbie?'

'Oh, nothing very original, I'm afraid. He fell in love with a twenty-two-year-old blonde and left his thirty-two-year-old wife.'

'Silly man. He should have had an affair with the twenty-two-year-old blonde and remained faithful to his thirty-two-year-old wife.'

'Isn't that a contradiction in terms?'

'Oh, no, I don't think so. I've never thought it unnatural to desire someone else. After all, it's a long life to go through and be expected never to want another woman.'

'I'm not so sure I agree with you,' said Debbie thoughtfully. 'I would like to have remained faithful to one man.'

Oh hell, thought Michael, not a very auspicious philosophy.

'Do you miss him?' he tried again.

'Yes, sometimes. It's true what they say in the glossy menopause magazines, one can be very lonely when you suddenly find yourself on your own.'

That sounds more promising, thought Michael, and he heard himself saying: 'Yes, I can understand that, but someone like you shouldn't have to stay on your own for very long.'

Debbie made no reply.

Michael refilled her glass of wine nearly to the brim, hoping he could order a second bottle before she finished her veal.

'Are you trying to get me drunk, Michael?'

'If you think it will help,' he replied laughing.

Debbie didn't laugh. Michael tried again.

'Been to the theatre lately?'

'Yes, I went to *Evita* last week. I loved it' — wonder who took you, thought Michael — 'but my mother fell asleep in the middle of the second act. I think I shall have to go and see it on my own a second time.'

'I only wish I was staying long enough to take you.'

'That would be fun,' she said.

'Whereas I shall have to be satisfied with seeing the show in London.'

'With your wife.'

'Another bottle of wine please, waiter.'

'No more for me, Michael, really.'

'Well, you can help me out a little.' The waiter faded away. 'Do you get to England at all yourself?' asked Michael.

'No, I've only been once when Roger, my ex, took the whole family. I loved the country. It fulfilled every one of my hopes but I'm afraid we did what all Americans are expected to do. The Tower of London, Buckingham Palace, followed by Oxford and Stratford, before flying on to Paris.'

'A sad way to see England; there's so much more I could have shown you.'

'I suspect when the English come to America

they don't see much outside of New York, Washington, Los Angeles, and perhaps San Francisco.'

'I agree,' said Michael, not wanting to disagree. The waiter cleared away their empty plates.

'Can I tempt you with a dessert, Debbie?'

'No, no, I'm trying to lose some weight.' Michael slipped a hand gently around her waist. 'You don't need to,' he said. 'You feel just perfect.'

She laughed. He smiled.

'Nevertheless, I'll stick to coffee, please.'

'A little brandy?'

'No, thank you, just coffee.'

'Black?'

'Black.'

'Coffee for two, please,' Michael said to the hovering waiter.

'I wish I had taken you somewhere a little quieter and less ostentatious,' he said, turning back to Debbie.

'Why?'

Michael took her hand. It felt cold. 'I would like to have said things to you that shouldn't be listened to by people on the next table.'

'I don't think anyone would be shocked by what they overheard at Elaine's, Michael.'

'Very well then. Do you believe in love at first sight?'

'No, but I think it's possible to be physically attracted to a person on first meeting them.'

'Well I must confess, I was to you.'

Again she made no reply.

The coffee arrived and Debbie released her hand to take a sip. Michael followed suit.

'There were one hundred and fifty women in that room the night we met, Debbie, and my eyes never left you once.'

'Even during the film?'

'I'd seen the damn thing a hundred times. I feared I might never see you again.'

'I'm touched.'

'Why should you be? It must be happening to you all the time.'

'Now and then,' she said. 'But I haven't taken anyone too seriously since my husband left me.'

'I'm sorry.'

'No need. It's just not that easy to get over someone you've lived with for ten years. I doubt if many divorcees are quite that willing to jump into bed with the first man who comes along as all the latest films suggest.'

Michael took her hand again, hoping fervently he did not fall into that category.

'It's been such a lovely evening. Why don't we stroll down to the Carlyle and listen to Bobby Short?' Michael's ABC friend had recommended the move if he felt he was still in with a chance.

'Yes, I'd enjoy that,' said Debbie.

Michael called for the bill — eighty-seven dollars. Had it been his wife sitting on the other side of the table he would have checked each item carefully, but not on this occasion. He just left five twenty-dollar bills on a side plate and didn't wait for the change. As they stepped out on to 2nd Avenue, he took Debbie's hand and together they started walking downtown. On

Madison Avenue they stopped in front of shop windows and he bought her a fur coat, a Cartier watch and a Balenciaga dress. Debbie thought it was lucky that all the stores were closed.

They arrived at the Carlyle just in time for the eleven o'clock show. A waiter, flashing a pen torch, guided them through the little dark room on the ground floor to a table in the corner. Michael ordered a bottle of champagne as Bobby Short struck up a chord and drawled out the words: 'Georgia, Georgia, oh, my sweet . . . ' Michael, now unable to speak to Debbie above the noise of the band, satisfied himself with holding her hand and when the entertainer sang, 'This time we almost made the pieces fit, didn't we, gal?' he leaned over and kissed her on the cheek. She turned and smiled — was it faintly conspiratorial, or was he just wishful thinking? — and then she sipped her champagne. On the dot of twelve, Bobby Short shut the piano lid and said, 'Goodnight, my friends, the time has come for all you good people to go to bed — and some of you naughty ones too.' Michael laughed a little too loud but was pleased that Debbie laughed as well.

They strolled down Madison Avenue to 68th Street chatting about inconsequential affairs, while Michael's thoughts were of only one affair. When they arrived at her 68th Street apartment, she took out her latch key.

'Would you like a nightcap?' she asked without any suggestive intonation.

'No more drink, thank you, Debbie, but I would certainly appreciate a coffee.'

She led him into the living room.

'The flowers have lasted well,' she teased, and left him to make the coffee. Michael amused himself by flicking through an old copy of *Time* magazine, looking at the pictures, not taking in the words. She returned after a few minutes with a coffee pot and two small cups on a lacquered tray. She poured the coffee, black again, and then sat down next to Michael on the couch, drawing one leg underneath her while turning slightly towards him. Michael downed his coffee in two gulps, scalding his mouth slightly. Then, putting down his cup, he leaned over and kissed her on the mouth. She was still clutching on to her coffee cup. Her eyes opened briefly as she manoeuvred the cup on to a side table. After another long kiss she broke away from him.

'I ought to make an early start in the morning.'

'So should I,' said Michael, 'but I am more worried about not seeing you again for a long time.'

'What a nice thing to say,' Debbie replied.

'No, I just care,' he said, before kissing her again.

This time she responded; he slipped one hand on to her breast while the other one began to undo the row of little buttons down the back of her dress. She broke away again.

'Don't let's do anything we'll regret.'

'I know we won't regret it,' said Michael.

He then kissed her on the neck and shoulders, slipping her dress off as he moved deftly down her body to her breast, delighted to find she wasn't wearing a bra.

'Shall we go upstairs, Debbie? I'm too old to make love on the sofa.'

Without speaking, she rose and led him by the hand to her bedroom, which smelled faintly and deliciously of the scent she herself was wearing.

She switched on a small bedside light and took off the rest of her clothes, letting them fall where she stood. Michael never once took his eyes off her body as he undressed clumsily on the other side of the bed. He slipped under the sheets and quickly joined her. When they had finished making love, an experience he hadn't enjoyed as much for a long time, he lay there pondering on the fact that she had succumbed at all, especially on their first date.

They lay silently in each other's arms before making love for a second time, which was every bit as delightful as the first. Michael then fell into a deep sleep.

He woke first the next morning and stared across at the beautiful woman who lay by his side. The digital clock on the bedside table showed seven-o-three. He touched her forehead lightly with his lips and began to stroke her hair. She woke lazily and smiled up at him. Then they made morning love, slowly, gently, but every bit as pleasing as the night before. He didn't speak as she slipped out of bed and ran a bath for him before going to the kitchen to prepare breakfast. Michael relaxed in the hot bath, crooning a Bobby Short number at the top of his voice. How he wished that Adrian could see him now. He dried himself and dressed before joining

Debbie in the little kitchen where they shared breakfast together. Eggs, bacon, toast, English marmalade, and steaming black coffee. Debbie then had a bath and dressed while Michael read the *New York Times*. When she reappeared in the living room wearing a smart coral dress, he was sorry to be leaving so soon.

'We must leave now, or you'll miss your flight.'

Michael rose reluctantly and Debbie drove him back to his hotel, where he quickly threw his clothes into a suitcase, settled the bill for his unslept-in double bed and joined her back in the car. On the journey to the airport they chatted about the coming elections and pumpkin pie almost as if they had been married for years or were both avoiding admitting the previous night had ever happened.

Debbie dropped Michael in front of the Pan Am building and put the car in the parking lot before joining him at the check-in counter. They waited for his flight to be called.

'Pan American announces the departure of their Flight Number 006 to London Heathrow. Will all passengers please proceed with their boarding passes to Gate Number Nine?'

When they reached the 'passengers-only' barrier, Michael took Debbie briefly in his arms. 'Thank you for a memorable evening,' he said.

'No, it is I who must thank you, Michael,' she replied as she kissed him on the cheek.

'I must confess I hadn't thought it would end up quite like that,' he said.

'Why not?' she asked.

'Not easy to explain,' he replied, searching for

words that would flatter and not embarrass. 'Let's say I was surprised that . . . '

'You were surprised that we ended up in bed together on our first night? You shouldn't be.'

'I shouldn't?'

'No, there's a simple enough explanation. My friends all told me when I got divorced to find myself a man and have a one-night stand. The idea sounded fun, but I didn't like the thought of the men in New York thinking I was easy.' She touched him gently on the side of his face. 'So when I met you and Adrian, both safely living over three thousand miles away, I thought to myself, 'whichever one of you comes back first' . . . '

A Chapter of Accidents

We first met Patrick Travers on our annual winter holiday to Verbier. We were waiting at the ski lift that first Saturday morning when a man who must have been in his early forties stood aside to allow Caroline to take his place, so that we could travel up together. He explained that he had already completed two runs that morning and didn't mind waiting. I thanked him and thought nothing more of it.

As soon as we reach the top my wife and I always go our separate ways, she to the A-slope to join Marcel, who only instructs advanced skiers — she has been skiing since the age of seven — I to the B-slope and any instructor who is available — I took up skiing at the age of forty-one, and frankly the B-slope is still too advanced for me though I don't dare admit as much, especially to Caroline. We always meet up again at the ski lift after completing our different runs.

That evening we bumped into Travers at the hotel bar. Since he seemed to be on his own we invited him to join us for dinner. He proved to be an amusing companion and we passed a pleasant enough evening together. He flirted politely with my wife without ever overstepping the mark, and she appeared to be flattered by his attentions. Over the years I have become used to men being attracted to Caroline, and I never need reminding how lucky I am. During dinner we learned that Travers was a merchant banker with an office in the City and a flat in Eaton Square. He had come to Verbier every year since he had been taken on a school trip in the late fifties, he told us. He still prided himself on being the first on the ski lift every morning, almost always beating the local blades up and down.

Travers appeared to be genuinely interested in the fact that I ran a small West End art gallery; as it turned out, he was something of a collector himself, specialising in minor Impressionists. He promised he would drop by and see my next exhibition when he was back in London.

I assured him that he would be most welcome but never gave it a second thought. In fact I only saw Travers a couple of times over the rest of the holiday, once talking to the wife of a friend of mine who owned a gallery that specialises in Oriental rugs, and later I noticed him following Caroline expertly down the treacherous A-slope.

* * *

It was six weeks later, and some minutes before I could place him that night at my gallery. I had to rack that part of one's memory which recalls names, a skill politicians rely on every day.

'Good to see you, Edward,' he said. 'I saw the write-up you got in the *Independent* and remembered your kind invitation to the private view.'

'Glad you could make it, Patrick,' I replied,

remembering just in time.

'I'm not a champagne man myself,' he told me, 'but I'll travel a long way to see a Vuillard.'

'You think highly of him?'

'Oh yes. I would compare him favourably with Pissarro and Bonnard, and he still remains one of the most under-rated of the Impressionists.'

'I agree,' I replied. 'But my gallery has felt that way about Vuillard for some considerable time.'

'How much is 'The Lady at the Window'?' he asked.

'Eighty thousand pounds,' I said quietly.

'It reminds me of a picture of his in the Metropolitan,' he said, as he studied the reproduction in the catalogue.

I was impressed, and told Travers that the Vuillard in New York had been painted within a month of the one he so admired.

He nodded. 'And the small nude?'

'Forty-seven thousand,' I told him.

'Mrs Hensell, the wife of his dealer and Vuillard's second mistress, if I'm not mistaken. The French are always so much more civilised about these things than we are. But my favourite painting in this exhibition,' he continued, 'compares surely with the finest of his work.' He turned to face the large oil of a young girl playing a piano, her mother bending to turn a page of the score.

'Magnificent,' he said. 'Dare I ask how much?'

'Three hundred and seventy thousand pounds,' I said, wondering if such a price tag put it out of Travers's bracket.

'What a super party, Edward,' said a voice

from behind my shoulder.

'Percy!' I cried, turning round. 'I thought you said you wouldn't be able to make it.'

'Yes, I did, old fellow, but I decided I couldn't sit at home alone all the time, so I've come to drown my sorrows in champagne.'

'Quite right too,' I said. 'Sorry to hear about Diana,' I added as Percy moved on. When I turned back to continue my conversation with Patrick Travers he was nowhere to be seen. I searched around the room and spotted him standing in the far corner of the gallery chatting to my wife, a glass of champagne in his hand. She was wearing an off-the-shoulder green dress that I considered a little too modern. Travers's eyes seemed to be glued to a spot a few inches below the shoulders. I would have thought nothing of it had he spoken to anyone else that evening.

The next occasion on which I saw Travers was about a week later on returning from the bank with some petty cash. Once again he was standing in front of the Vuillard oil of mother and daughter at the piano.

'Good morning, Patrick,' I said as I joined him.

'I can't seem to get that picture out of my mind,' he declared, as he continued to stare at the two figures.

'Understandably.'

'I don't suppose you would allow me to live with them for a week or two until I can finally make up my mind? Naturally I would be quite happy to leave a deposit.'

'Of course,' I said. 'I would require a bank reference as well and the deposit would be twenty-five thousand pounds.'

He agreed to both requests without hesitation, so I asked him where he would like the picture delivered. He handed me a card which revealed his address in Eaton Square. The following morning his bankers confirmed that three hundred and seventy thousand pounds would not be a problem for their client.

Within twenty-four hours the Vuillard had been taken round to his home and hung in the dining room on the ground floor. He phoned in the afternoon to thank me, and asked if Caroline and I would care to join him for dinner; he wanted, he said, a second opinion on how the painting looked.

With three hundred and seventy thousand pounds at stake I didn't feel it was an invitation I could reasonably turn down, and in any case Caroline seemed eager to accept, explaining that she was interested to see what his house was like.

We dined with Travers the following Thursday. We turned out to be the only guests, and I remember being surprised that there wasn't a Mrs Travers or at least a resident girlfriend. He was a thoughtful host and the meal he had arranged was superb. However, I considered at the time that he seemed a little too solicitous towards Caroline, although she certainly gave the impression of enjoying his undivided attention. At one point I began to wonder if either of them would have noticed if I had disappeared into thin air.

When we left Eaton Square that night Travers told me that he had almost made up his mind about the picture, which made me feel the evening had served at least some purpose.

Six days later the painting was returned to the gallery with a note attached explaining that he no longer cared for it. Travers did not elaborate on his reasons, but simply ended by saying that he hoped to drop by some time and reconsider the other Vuillards. Disappointed, I returned his deposit, but realised that customers often do come back, sometimes months, even years later.

But Travers never did.

It was about a month later that I learned why he would never return. I was lunching at the large centre table at my club, as in most all-male establishments the table reserved for members who drift in on their own. Percy Fellows was the next to enter the dining room, and he took a seat opposite me. I hadn't seen him to talk to since the private view of the Vuillard exhibition and we hadn't really had much of a conversation then. Percy was one of the most respected antique dealers in England, and I had once even done a successful barter with him, a Charles II writing desk in exchange for a Dutch landscape by Utrillo.

I repeated how sorry I was to learn about Diana.

'It was always going to end in divorce,' he explained. 'She was in and out of every bedroom in London. I was beginning to look a complete cuckold, and that bloody man Travers was the last straw.'

'Travers?' I said, not understanding.

'Patrick Travers, the man named in my divorce petition. Ever come across him?'

'I know the name,' I said hesitantly, wanting to hear more before I admitted to our slight acquaintance.

'Funny,' he said. 'Could have sworn I saw him at the private view.'

'But what do you mean, he was the last straw?' I asked, trying to take his mind off the opening.

'Met the bloody fellow at Ascot, didn't we? Joined us for lunch, happily drank my champagne, ate my strawberries and cream and then before the week was out had bedded my wife. But that's not the half of it.'

'The half of it?'

'The man had the nerve to come round to my shop and put down a large deposit on a Georgian table. Then he invites the two of us round to dinner to see how it looks. After he's had enough time to make love to Diana he returns them both slightly soiled. You don't look too well, old fellow,' said Percy suddenly. 'Something wrong with the food? Never been the same since Harry left for the Carlton. I've written to the wine committee about it several times, but — '

'No, I'm fine,' I said. 'I just need a little fresh air. Please excuse me, Percy.'

It was on the walk back from my club that I decided I would have to do something about Mr Travers.

* * *

The next morning I waited for the mail to arrive and checked any envelopes addressed to Caroline. Nothing seemed untoward, but then I decided that Travers wouldn't have been foolish enough to commit anything to paper. I also began to eavesdrop on her telephone conversations, but he was not among the callers, at least not while I was at home. I even checked the mileometer on her Mini to see if she had driven any long distances, but then Eaton Square isn't all that far. It's often what you don't do that gives the game away, I decided: we didn't make love for a fortnight, and she didn't comment.

I continued to watch Caroline more carefully over the next few weeks, but it became obvious to me that Travers must have tired of her about the same time as he had returned the Vuillard. This only made me more angry.

I then formed a plan of revenge that seemed quite extraordinary to me at the time, and I assumed that in a matter of days I would get over it, even forget it. But I didn't. If anything, the idea grew into an obsession. I began to convince myself that it was my bounden duty to do away with Travers before he besmirched any more of my friends.

I have never in my life knowingly broken the law. Parking fines annoy me, dropped litter offends me and I pay my VAT on the same day the frightful buff envelope drops through the letterbox.

Nevertheless, once I'd decided what had to be done I set about my task meticulously. At first I considered shooting Travers, until I discovered how hard it is to get a gun licence, and that if I did the job properly he would end up feeling very little pain, which wasn't what I had planned for him. Then poisoning crossed my mind — but that requires a witnessed prescription, and I still wouldn't be able to watch the long slow death I desired. Then strangling, which I decided would necessitate too much courage — and in any case he was a bigger man than me so *I* might end up being the one who was strangled. Then drowning, which could take years to get the man near any water, and then I might not be able to hang around to make sure he went under for the third time. I even gave some thought to running over the damned man, but dropped that idea when I realised opportunity would be almost nil and besides, I wouldn't be left any time to check if he was dead. I was quickly becoming aware just how hard it is to kill someone — and get away with it.

I sat awake at night reading the biographies of murderers, but as they had all been caught and found guilty that didn't fill me with much confidence. I turned to detective novels, which always seemed to allow for a degree of coincidence, luck and surprise that I was unwilling to risk, until I came across a rewarding line from Conan Doyle: 'Any intended victim who has a regular routine immediately makes himself more vulnerable.' And then I recalled one routine of which Travers was particularly proud. It required a further six-month wait on my part, but that gave me more time to perfect my plan. I used the enforced wait well because whenever Caroline was away for more than twenty-four hours, I booked in for a skiing lesson on the dry slope at Harrow.

I found it surprisingly easy to discover when Travers would be returning to Verbier, and I was able to organise the winter holiday so that our paths would cross for only three days, a period of time quite sufficient for me to commit my first crime.

* * *

Caroline and I arrived in Verbier on the second Friday in January. She had commented on the state of my nerves more than once over the Christmas period, and hoped the holiday would help me relax. I could hardly explain to her that it was the thought of the holiday that was making me so tense. It didn't help when she asked me on the plane to Switzerland if I thought Travers might be there this year.

On the first morning after our arrival we took the ski lift up at about ten-thirty, and once we had reached the top, Caroline duly reported to Marcel. As she departed with him for the A-slope I returned to the B-slope to work on my own. As always we agreed to meet back at the ski lift or, if we missed each other, at least for lunch.

During the days that followed I went over and over the plan I had perfected in my mind and practised so diligently at Harrow until I felt sure it was foolproof. By the end of the first week I had convinced myself I was ready.

* * *

The night before Travers was due to arrive I was the last to leave the slopes. Even Caroline commented on how much my skiing had improved, and she suggested to Marcel that I was ready for the A-slope with its sharper bends and steeper inclines.

'Next year, perhaps,' I told her, trying to make light of it, and returned to the B-slope.

During the final morning I skied over the first mile of the course again and again, and became so preoccupied with my work that I quite forgot to join Caroline for lunch.

In the afternoon I checked and rechecked the placing of every red flag marking the run, and once I was convinced the last skier had left the slope for the evening I collected about thirty of the flags and replaced them at intervals I had carefully worked out. My final task was to check the prepared patch before building a large mound of snow some twenty paces above the chosen spot. Once my preparations were complete I skied slowly down the mountain in the fading light.

'Are you trying to win an Olympic gold medal or something?' Caroline asked me when I eventually got back to our room. I closed the bathroom door so she couldn't expect a reply.

Travers checked in to the hotel an hour later.

I waited until the early evening before I joined him at the bar for a drink. He seemed a little nervous when he first saw me, but I quickly put him at ease. His old self-confidence soon returned, which only made me more determined to carry out my plan. I left him at the bar a few minutes before Caroline came down for dinner so that she wouldn't see the two of us together. Innocent surprise would be necessary once the deed had been done.

'Unlike you to eat so little, especially as you missed your lunch,' Caroline remarked as we left the dining room that night.

I made no comment as we passed Travers seated at the bar, his hand on the knee of another innocent middle-aged woman.

I did not sleep for one second that night and I crept out of bed just before six the next morning, careful not to wake Caroline. Everything was laid out on the bathroom floor just as I had left it the night before. A few moments later I was dressed and ready. I walked down the back stairs of the hotel, avoiding the lift, and crept out by the fire exit, realising for the first time what a thief must feel like. I had a woollen cap pulled well down over my ears and a pair of snow goggles covering my eyes: not even Caroline would have recognised me.

I arrived at the bottom of the ski lift forty minutes before it was due to open. As I stood alone behind the little shed that housed the electrical machinery to work the lift I realised that everything now depended on Travers's sticking to his routine. I wasn't sure I could go through with it if my plan had to be moved on to the following day. As I waited, I stamped my feet in the freshly fallen snow, and slapped my arms around my chest to keep warm. Every few moments I kept peering round the corner of the building in the hope that I would see him striding towards me. At last a speck appeared at the bottom of the hill by the side of the road, a pair of skis resting on the man's shoulders. But what if it turned out not to be Travers?

I stepped out from behind the shed a few moments later to join the warmly wrapped man. It *was* Travers, and he could not hide his surprise at seeing me standing there. I started up a casual conversation about being unable to sleep, and how I thought I might as well put in a few runs before the rush began. Now all I needed was the ski lift to start up on time. A few minutes after seven an engineer arrived and the vast oily mechanism cranked into action.

We were the first two to take our places on those little seats before heading up and over the deep ravine. I kept turning back to check there was still no one else in sight.

'I usually manage to complete a full run even before the second person arrives,' Travers told me when the lift had reached its highest point. I looked back again to be sure we were now well out of sight of the engineer working the lift, then peered down some two hundred feet and wondered what it would be like to land head first in the ravine. I began to feel dizzy and wished I hadn't looked down.

The ski lift jerked slowly on up the icy wire until we finally reached the landing point.

'Damn,' I said, as we jumped off our little seats. 'Marcel isn't here.'

'Never is at this time,' said Travers, making off

towards the advanced slope. 'Far too early for him.'

'I don't suppose you would come down with me?' I said, calling after Travers.

He stopped and looked back suspiciously.

'Caroline thinks I'm ready to join you,' I explained, 'but I'm not so sure and would value a second opinion. I've broken my own record for the B-slope several times, but I wouldn't want to make a fool of myself in front of my wife.'

'Well, I — '

'I'd ask Marcel if he were here. And in any case you're the best skier I know.'

'Well, if you — ' he began.

'Just the once, then you can spend the rest of your holiday on the A-slope. You could even treat the run as a warm-up.'

'Might make a change, I suppose,' he said.

'Just the once,' I repeated. 'That's all I'll need. Then you'll be able to tell me if I'm good enough.'

'Shall we make a race of it?' he said, taking me by surprise just as I began clamping on my skis. I couldn't complain; all the books on murder had warned me to be prepared for the unexpected. 'That's one way we can find out if you're ready,' he added cockily.

'If you insist. Don't forget, I'm older and less experienced than you,' I reminded him. I checked my skis quickly because I knew I had to start off in front of him.

'But you know the B-course backwards,' he retorted. 'I've never even seen it before.'

'I'll agree to a race, but only if you'll consider a wager,' I replied.

For the first time I could see I had caught his interest. 'How much?' he asked.

'Oh, nothing so vulgar as money,' I said. 'The winner gets to tell Caroline the truth.'

'The truth?' he said, looking puzzled.

'Yes,' I replied, and shot off down the hill before he could respond. I got a good start as I skied in and out of the red flags, but looking back over my shoulder I could see he had recovered quickly and was already chasing hard after me. I realised that it was vital for me to stay in front of him for the first third of the course, but I could already feel him cutting down my lead.

After half a mile of swerving and driving he shouted, 'You'll have to go a lot faster than that if you hope to beat me.' His arrogant boast only pushed me to stay ahead, but I kept the lead only because of my advantage of knowing every twist and turn during that first mile. Once I was sure that I would reach the vital newly marked route before he could I began to relax. After all, I had practised over the next two hundred metres fifty times a day for the last ten days, but I was only too aware that this time was the only one that mattered.

I glanced over my shoulder to see he was now about thirty metres behind me. I began to slow slightly as we approached the prepared ice patch, hoping he wouldn't notice or would think I'd lost my nerve. I held back even more when I reached the top of the patch until I could almost feel the sound of his breathing. Then, quite suddenly, the moment before I would have hit the ice I ploughed my skis and came to a complete halt in the mound of snow I had built the previous night. Travers sailed past me at about forty miles an hour, and seconds later flew high into the air over the ravine with a scream I will never forget. I couldn't get myself to look over the edge, as I knew he must have broken every bone in his body the moment he hit the snow a hundred feet below.

I carefully levelled the mound of snow that had saved my life and then clambered back up the mountain as fast as I could go, gathering the thirty flags that had marked out my false route. Then I skied from side to side replacing them in their correct positions on the B-slope, some hundred metres above my carefully prepared ice patch. When each one was back in place I skied on down the hill, feeling like an Olympic champion. Once I reached the base of the slope I pulled up my hood to cover my head, and didn't remove my snow goggles. I unstrapped my skis and walked casually towards the hotel. I re-entered the building by the rear door and was back in bed by seven-forty.

I tried to control my breathing, but it was some time before my pulse had returned to normal. Caroline woke a few minutes later, turned over and put her arms round me.

'Ugh,' she said, 'you're frozen. Have you been sleeping without the covers on?'

I laughed. 'You must have pulled them off during the night.'

‘Go and have a hot bath.’

After I had had a quick bath we made love and I dressed a second time, double-checking that I had left no clues of my early flight before going down to breakfast.

As Caroline was pouring my second cup of coffee, I heard the ambulance siren, at first coming from the town and then later returning.

‘Hope it wasn’t a bad accident,’ my wife said as she continued to pour her coffee.

‘What?’ I said, a little too loudly, glancing up from the previous day’s *Times*.

‘The siren, silly. There must have been an accident on the mountain. Probably Travers,’ she said.

‘Travers?’ I said, even more loudly.

‘Patrick Travers. I saw him at the bar last night. I didn’t mention it to you because I know you don’t care for him.’

‘But why Travers?’ I asked nervously.

‘Doesn’t he always claim he’s the first on the slope every morning? Even beats the instructors up to the top.’

‘Does he?’ I said.

‘You must remember. We were going up for the first time the day we met him, and he was already on his third run.’

‘Was he?’

‘You are being dim this morning, Edward. Did you get out of bed the wrong side?’ she asked, laughing.

I didn’t reply.

‘Well, I only hope it *is* Travers,’ Caroline added, sipping her coffee. ‘I never did like the man.’

'Why not?' I asked, somewhat taken aback.

'He once made a pass at me,' she said casually.

I stared across at her, unable to speak.

'Aren't you going to ask what happened?'

'I'm so stunned I don't know what to say,' I replied.

'He was all over me at the gallery that night, and then invited me out to lunch after we had dinner with him. I told him to get lost,' Caroline said. She touched me gently on the hand. 'I've never mentioned it to you before because I thought it might have been the reason he returned the Vuillard, and that only made me feel guilty.'

'But it's me who should feel guilty,' I said, fumbling with a piece of toast.

'Oh, no, darling, you're not guilty of anything. In any case, if I ever decided to be unfaithful it wouldn't be with a lounge lizard like that. Good heavens no. Diana had already warned me what to expect from him. Not my style at all.'

I sat there thinking of Travers on his way to a morgue, or even worse, still buried under the snow, knowing there was nothing I could do about it.

'You know, I think the time really has come for you to tackle the A-slope,' Caroline said as we finished breakfast. 'Your skiing has improved beyond words.'

'Yes,' I replied, more than a little preoccupied.

I hardly spoke another word as we made our way together to the foot of the mountain.

'Are you all right, darling?' Caroline asked as we travelled up side by side on the lift.

'Fine,' I said, unable to look down into the ravine as we reached the highest point. Was Travers still down there, or already in the morgue?

'Stop looking like a frightened child. After all the work you've put in this week you're more than ready to join me,' she said reassuringly.

I smiled weakly. When we reached the top, I jumped off the ski lift just a moment too early, and knew as soon as I took my second step that I had sprained an ankle.

I received no sympathy from Caroline. She was convinced I was putting it on in order to avoid attempting the advanced run. She swept past me and sped on down the mountain while I returned in ignominy via the lift. When I reached the bottom I glanced towards the engineer, but he didn't give me a second look. I hobbled over to the first aid post and checked in. Caroline joined me a few minutes later.

I explained to her that the duty orderly thought it might be a fracture and had suggested I report to the hospital immediately.

Caroline frowned, removed her skis and went off to find a taxi to take us to the hospital. It wasn't a long journey but it was one the taxi driver had evidently done many times before from the way he took the slippery bends.

'I ought to be able to dine out on this for about a year,' Caroline promised me as we entered the double doors of the hospital.

'Would you be kind enough to wait outside, madam?' asked a male orderly as I was ushered into the X-ray room.

'Yes, but will I ever see my poor husband again?' she mocked as the door was closed in front of her.

I entered a room full of sophisticated machinery presided over by an expensively dressed doctor. I told him what I thought was wrong with me and he lifted the offending foot gently up on to an X-ray machine. Moments later he was studying the large negative.

'There's no fracture there,' he assured me, pointing to the bone. 'But if you are still in any pain it might be wise for me to bind the ankle up tightly.' He pinned my X-ray next to five others hanging from a rail.

'Am I the sixth person already today?' I asked, looking up at the row of X-rays.

'No, no,' he said, laughing. 'The other five are all the same man. I think he must have tried to fly over the ravine, the fool.'

'Over the ravine?'

'Yes, showing off, I suspect,' he said as he began to bind my ankle. 'We get one every year, but this poor fellow broke both his legs and an arm, and will have a nasty scar on his face to remind him of his stupidity. Lucky to be alive, in my opinion.'

'Lucky to be alive?' I repeated weakly.

'Yes, but only because he didn't know what he was doing. My fourteen-year-old skis over that ravine and can land like a seagull on water. He, on the other hand,' the doctor pointed to the X-rays, 'won't be skiing again this holiday. In fact, he won't be walking for at least six months.'

'Really?' I said.

'And as for you,' he added, after he finished binding me up, 'just rest the ankle in ice every three hours and change the bandage once a day. You should be back on the slopes again in a couple of days, three at the most.'

'We're flying back this evening,' I told him as I gingerly got to my feet.

'Good timing,' he said, smiling.

I hobbled happily out of the X-ray room to find Caroline head down in *Elle*.

'You look pleased with yourself,' she said, looking up.

'I am. It turns out to be nothing worse than two broken legs, a broken arm and a scar on the face.'

'How stupid of me,' said Caroline, 'I thought it was a simple sprain.'

'Not me,' I told her. 'Travers — the accident this morning, you remember? The ambulance. Still, they assure me he'll live,' I added.

'Pity,' she said, linking her arm through mine. 'After all the trouble you took, I was rather hoping you'd succeed.'

Checkmate

As she entered the room every eye turned towards her.

When admiring a girl some men start with her head and work down. I start with the ankles and work up.

She wore black high-heeled velvet shoes and a tight-fitting black dress that stopped high enough above the knees to reveal the most perfectly tapering legs. As my eyes continued their upward sweep they paused to take in her narrow waist and slim athletic figure. But it was the oval face that I found captivating, slightly pouting lips and the largest blue eyes I've ever seen, crowned with a head of thick, black, short-cut hair that literally shone with lustre. Her entrance was all the more breath-taking because of the surroundings she had chosen. Heads would have turned at a diplomatic reception, a society cocktail party, even a charity ball, but at a chess tournament . . .

I followed her every movement, patronisingly unable to accept she could be a player. She walked slowly over to the club secretary's table and signed in to prove me wrong. She was handed a number to indicate her challenger for the opening match. Anyone who had not yet been allocated an opponent waited to see if she would take her place opposite their side of the board.

The player checked the number she had been given and made her way towards an elderly man who was seated in the far corner of the room, a former captain of the club now past his best.

As the club's new captain I had been responsible for instigating these round-robin matches. We meet on the last Friday of the month in a large club-like room on top of the Mason's Arms in the High Street. The landlord sees to it that thirty tables are set out for us and that food and drink are readily available. Three or four other clubs in the district send half a dozen opponents to play a couple of blitz games, giving us a chance to face rivals we would not normally play. The rules for the matches are simple enough — one minute on the clock is the maximum allowed for each move, so a game rarely lasts for more than an hour, and if a pawn hasn't been captured in thirty moves the game is automatically declared a draw. A short break for a drink between games, paid for by the loser, ensures that everyone has the chance to challenge two opponents during the evening.

A thin man wearing half-moon spectacles and a dark blue three-piece suit made his way over towards my board. We smiled and shook hands. My guess would have been a solicitor, but I was wrong as he turned out to be an accountant working for a stationery supplier in Woking.

I found it hard to concentrate on my opponent's well-rehearsed Moscow opening as my eyes kept leaving the board and wandering over to the girl in the black dress. On the one occasion our eyes did meet she gave me an enigmatic smile, but although I tried again I was unable to elicit the same response a second time. Despite being preoccupied I still managed to defeat the accountant, who seemed unaware that there were several ways out of a seven-pawn attack.

At the half-time break three other members of the club had offered her a drink before I even reached the bar. I knew I could not hope to play my second match against the girl as I would be expected to challenge one of the visiting team captains. In fact she ended up playing the accountant.

I defeated my new opponent in a little over forty minutes and, as a solicitous host, began to take an interest in the other matches that were still being played. I set out on a circuitous route that ensured I ended up at her table. I could see that the accountant already had the better of her, and within moments of my arrival she had lost both her queen and the game.

I introduced myself and found that just shaking hands with her was a sexual experience. Weaving our way through the tables we strolled over to the bar together. Her name, she told me, was Amanda Curzon. I ordered Amanda the glass of red wine she requested and a half-pint of beer for myself. I began by commiserating with her over the defeat.

'How did you get on against him?' she asked.

'Just managed to beat him,' I said. 'But it was very close. How did your first game with our old captain turn out?'

'Stalemate,' said Amanda. 'But I think he was

just being courteous.'

'Last time I played him it ended up in stalemate,' I told her.

She smiled. 'Perhaps we ought to have a game some time?'

'I'll look forward to that,' I said, as she finished her drink.

'Well, I must be off,' she announced suddenly. 'Have to catch the last train to Hounslow.'

'Allow me to drive you,' I said gallantly. 'It's the least the host captain can be expected to do.'

'But surely it's miles out of your way?'

'Not at all,' I lied, Hounslow being about twenty minutes beyond my flat. I gulped down the last drop of my beer and helped Amanda on with her coat. Before leaving I thanked the landlord for the efficient organisation of the evening.

We then strolled into the car park. I opened the passenger door of my Scirocco to allow Amanda to climb in.

'A slight improvement on London Transport,' she said as I slid into my side of the car. I smiled and headed out on the road northwards. That black dress that I described earlier goes even higher up the legs when a girl sits back in a Scirocco. It didn't seem to embarrass her.

'It's still very early,' I ventured after a few inconsequential remarks about the club evening. 'Have you time to drop in for a drink?'

'It would have to be a quick one,' she replied, looking at her watch. 'I've a busy day ahead of me tomorrow.'

'Of course,' I said, chatting on, hoping she

wouldn't notice a detour that could hardly be described as on the way to Hounslow.

'Do you work in town?' I asked.

'Yes. I'm a receptionist for a firm of estate agents in Berkeley Square.'

'I'm surprised you're not a model.'

'I used to be,' she replied without further explanation. She seemed quite oblivious to the route I was taking as she chatted on about her holiday plans for Ibiza. Once we had arrived at my place I parked the car and led Amanda through my front gate and up to the flat. In the hall I helped her off with her coat before taking her through to the front room.

'What would you like to drink?' I asked.

'I'll stick to wine, if you've a bottle already open,' she replied, as she walked slowly round, taking in the unusually tidy room. My mother must have dropped by during the morning, I thought gratefully.

'It's only a bachelor pad,' I said, emphasising the word 'bachelor' before going into the kitchen. To my relief I found there was an unopened bottle of wine in the larder. I joined Amanda with the bottle and two glasses a few moments later, to find her studying my chess board and fingering the delicate ivory pieces that were set out for a game I was playing by post.

'What a beautiful set,' she volunteered as I handed her a glass of wine. 'Where did you find it?'

'Mexico,' I told her, not explaining that I had won it in a tournament while on holiday there. 'I was only sorry we didn't have the chance to have a game ourselves.'

She checked her watch. 'Time for a quick one,' she said, taking a seat behind the little white pieces.

I quickly took my place opposite her. She smiled, picked up a white and a black bishop and hid them behind her back. Her dress became even tighter and emphasised the shape of her breasts. She then placed both clenched fists in front of me. I touched her right hand and she turned it over and opened it to reveal a white bishop.

'Is there to be a wager of any kind?' I asked lightheartedly. She checked inside her evening bag.

'I only have a few pounds on me,' she said.

'I'd be willing to play for lower stakes.'

'What do you have in mind?' she asked.

'What can you offer?'

'What would you like?'

'Ten pounds if you win.'

'And if I lose?'

'You take something off.'

I regretted the words the moment I had said them and waited for her to slap my face and leave but she said simply, 'There's not much harm in that if we only play one game.'

I nodded my agreement and stared down at the board.

She wasn't a bad player — what the pros call a *patzer* — though her Roux opening was somewhat orthodox. I managed to make the game last twenty minutes while sacrificing several pieces without making it look too obvious. When I said 'Checkmate', she kicked off both her shoes and laughed.

'Care for another drink?' I asked, not feeling too hopeful. 'After all, it's not yet eleven.'

'All right. Just a small one and then I must be off.'

I went to the kitchen, returned a moment later clutching the bottle, and refilled her glass.

'I only wanted half a glass,' she said, frowning.

'I was lucky to win,' I said, ignoring her remark, 'after your bishop captured my knight. Extremely close-run thing.'

'Perhaps,' she replied.

'Care for another game?' I ventured.

She hesitated.

'Double or quits?'

'What do you mean?'

'Twenty pounds or another garment?'

'Neither of us is going to lose much tonight, are we?'

She pulled up her chair as I turned the board round and we both began to put the ivory pieces back in place.

The second game took a little longer as I made a silly mistake early on, castling on my queen's side, and it took several moves to recover. However, I still managed to finish the game off in under thirty minutes and even found time to refill Amanda's glass when she wasn't looking.

She smiled at me as she hitched her dress up high enough to allow me to see the tops of her stockings. She undid the suspenders and slowly peeled the stockings off before dropping them on my side of the table.

'I nearly beat you that time,' she said.

'Almost,' I replied. 'Want another chance to get even? Let's say fifty pounds this time,' I suggested, trying to make the offer sound magnanimous.

'The stakes are getting higher for both of us,' she replied as she reset the board. I began to wonder what might be going through her mind. Whatever it was, she foolishly sacrificed both her rooks early on and the game was over in a matter of minutes.

Once again she lifted her dress but this time well above her waist. My eyes were glued to her thighs as she undid the black suspender belt and held it high above my head before letting it drop and join her stockings on my side of the table.

'Once I had lost the second rook,' she said, 'I was never in with a chance.'

'I agree. It would therefore only be fair to allow you one more chance,' I said, quickly resetting the board. 'After all,' I added, 'you could win one hundred pounds this time.' She smiled.

'I really ought to be going home,' she said as she moved her queen's pawn two squares forward. She smiled that enigmatic smile again as I countered with my bishop's pawn.

It was the best game she had played all evening and her use of the Warsaw gambit kept me at the board for over thirty minutes. In fact I damn nearly lost early on because I found it hard to concentrate properly on her defence strategy. A couple of times Amanda chuckled when she thought she had got the better of me, but it became obvious she had not seen Karpov play the Sicilian defence and win from a seemingly impossible position.

'Checkmate,' I finally declared.

'Damn,' she said, and standing up turned her back on me. 'You'll have to give me a hand.' Trembling, I leaned over and slowly pulled the zip down until it reached the small of her back. Once again I wanted to touch the smooth, creamy skin. She swung round to face me, shrugged gracefully and the dress fell to the ground as if a statue were being unveiled. She leaned forward and brushed the side of my cheek with her hand, which had much the same effect as an electric shock. I emptied the last of the bottle of wine into her glass and left for the kitchen with the excuse of needing to refill my own. When I returned she hadn't moved. A gauzy black bra and pair of panties were now the only garments that I still hoped to see removed.

'I don't suppose you'd play one more game?' I asked, trying not to sound desperate.

'It's time you took me home,' she said with a giggle.

I passed her another glass of wine. 'Just one more,' I begged. 'But this time it must be for both garments.'

She laughed. 'Certainly not,' she said. 'I couldn't afford to lose.'

'It would have to be the last game,' I agreed. 'But two hundred pounds this time and we play for both garments.' I waited, hoping the size of the wager would tempt her. 'The odds must surely be on your side. After all, you've nearly won three times.'

She sipped her drink as if considering the proposition. 'All right,' she said. 'One last fling.'

Neither of us voiced our feeling as to what was certain to happen if she lost.

I could not stop myself trembling as I set the board up once again. I cleared my mind, hoping she hadn't noticed that I had drunk only one glass of wine all night. I was determined to finish this one off quickly.

I moved my queen's pawn one square forward. She retaliated, pushing her king's pawn up two squares. I knew exactly what my next move needed to be and because of it the game only lasted eleven minutes.

I have never been so comprehensively beaten in my life. Amanda was in a totally different class to me. She anticipated my every move and had gambits I had never encountered or even read of before.

It was her turn to say 'Checkmate,' which she delivered with the same enigmatic smile as before, adding, 'You did say the odds were on my side this time.'

I lowered my head in disbelief. When I looked up again, she had already slipped that beautiful black dress back on, and was stuffing her stockings and suspenders into her evening bag. A moment later she put on her shoes.

I took out my chequebook, filled in the name 'Amanda Curzon' and added the figure '£200', the date and my signature. While I was doing this she replaced the little ivory pieces on the exact squares on which they had been when she had first entered the room.

She bent over and kissed me gently on the cheek. 'Thank you,' she said as she placed the cheque in her handbag. 'We must play again some time.' I was still staring at the reset board in disbelief when I heard the front door close behind her.

'Wait a minute,' I said, rushing to the door. 'How will you get home?'

I was just in time to see her running down the steps and towards the open door of a BMW. She climbed in, allowing me one more look at those long tapering legs. She smiled as the car door was closed behind her.

The accountant strolled round to the driver's side, got in, revved up the engine and drove the champion home.

The Century

'Life is a game,' said A. T. Pierson, thus immortalising himself without actually having to do any real work. Though E. M. Forster showed more insight when he wrote 'Fate is the Umpire, and Hope is the Ball, which is why I will never score a century at Lord's.'

When I was a freshman at university, my room mate invited me to have dinner in a sporting club to which he belonged called Vincent's. Such institutions do not differ greatly around the Western world. They are always brimful of outrageously fit, healthy young animals, whose sole purpose in life seems to be to challenge the opposition of some neighbouring institution to ridiculous feats of physical strength. My host's main rivals, he told me with undergraduate fervour, came from a high-thinking, plain-living establishment which had dozed the unworldly centuries away in the flat, dull, fen country of England described on the map as Cambridge. Now the ultimate ambition of men such as my host was simple enough: in whichever sport they aspired to beat the 'Tabs' the select few were rewarded with a Blue. As there is no other way of gaining this distinction at either Oxford or Cambridge, every place in the team is contested for with considerable zeal. A man may be selected and indeed play in every other match of the season for the University, even go on to represent his country, but if he does not play in the Oxford and Cambridge match, he cannot describe himself as a Blue.

My story concerns a delightful character I met that evening when I dined as a guest at Vincent's. The undergraduate to whom I refer was in his final year. He came from that part of the world that we still dared to describe in those days (without a great deal of thought) as the colonies. He was an Indian by birth, and the son of a man whose name in England was a household word, if not a legend, for he had captained Oxford and India at cricket, which meant that outside of the British Commonwealth he was about as well known as Babe Ruth is to the English. The young man's father had added to his fame by scoring a century at Lord's when captaining the University cricket side against Cambridge. In fact, when he went on to captain India against England he used to take pride in wearing his cream sweater with the wide dark blue band around the neck and waist. The son, experts predicted, would carry on in the family tradition. He was in much the same mould as his father, tall and rangy with jet-black hair, and as a cricketer, a fine right-handed batsman and a useful left-arm spin bowler. (Those of you who have never been able to comprehend the English language let alone the game of cricket might well be tempted to ask why not a fine right-arm batsman and a useful left-handed spin bowler. The English, however, always cover such silly questions with the words: Tradition, dear boy, tradition.)

The young Indian undergraduate, like his father, had come up to Oxford with considerably more interest in defeating Cambridge than the examiners. As a freshman, he had played against most of the English county sides, notching up a century against three of them, and on one occasion taking five wickets in an innings. A week before the big match against Cambridge, the skipper informed him that he had won his Blue and that the names of the chosen eleven would be officially announced in *The Times* the following day. The young man telegraphed his father in Calcutta with the news, and then went off for a celebratory dinner at Vincent's. He entered the Club's dining room in high spirits to the traditional round of applause afforded to a new Blue, and as he was about to take a seat he observed the boat crew, all nine of them, around a circular table at the far end of the room. He walked across to the captain of boats and remarked: 'I thought you chaps sat one behind each other.'

Within seconds, four thirteen-stone men were sitting on the new Blue while the cox poured a jug of cold water over his head.

'If you fail to score a century,' said one oar, 'we'll use hot water next time.' When the four oars had returned to their table, the cricketer rose slowly, straightened his tie in mock indignation, and as he passed the crew's table, patted the five-foot-one-inch, 102-pound cox on the head and said, ‘Even losing teams should have a mascot.’

This time they only laughed but it was in the very act of patting the cox on the head that he first noticed his thumb felt a little bruised and he commented on the fact to the wicket-keeper who had joined him for dinner. A large entrecôte steak arrived and he found as he picked up his knife that he was unable to grip the handle properly. He tried to put the inconvenience out of his mind, assuming all would be well by the following morning. But the next day he woke in considerable pain and found to his dismay that the thumb was not only black but also badly swollen. After reporting the news to his captain he took the first available train to London for a consultation with a Harley Street specialist. As the carriage rattled through Berkshire, he read in *The Times* that he had been awarded his Blue.

The specialist studied the offending thumb for some considerable time and expressed his doubt that the young man would be able to hold a ball, let alone a bat, for at least a fortnight. The prognosis turned out to be accurate and our hero sat disconsolate in the stand at Lord’s, watching Oxford lose the match and the twelfth man gain his Blue. His father, who had flown over from Calcutta especially for the encounter, offered his condolences, pointing out that he still had two years left in which to gain the honour.

As his second Trinity term approached, even the young man forgot his disappointment and in the opening match of the season against Somerset scored a memorable century, full of cuts and drives that reminded *aficionados* of his father. The son had been made Secretary of cricket in the closed season as it was universally acknowledged that only bad luck and the boat crew had stopped him from reaping his just reward as a freshman. Once again, he played in every fixture before the needle match, but in the last four games against county teams he failed to score more than a dozen runs and did not take a single wicket, while his immediate rivals excelled themselves. He was going through a lean patch, and was the first to agree with his captain that with so much talent around that year he should not be risked against Cambridge. Once again he watched Oxford lose the Blues match and his opposite number the Cambridge Secretary, Robin Oakley, score a faultless century. A man well into his sixties sporting an MCC tie came up to the young Indian during the game, patted him on the shoulder, and remarked that he would never forget the day his father had scored a hundred against Cambridge: it didn't help.

When the cricketer returned for his final year, he was surprised and delighted to be selected by his team-mates to be captain, an honour never previously afforded to a man who had not been awarded the coveted Blue. His peers recognised his outstanding work as Secretary and knew if he could reproduce the form of his freshman year he would undoubtedly not only win a Blue but go on to represent his country.

The tradition at Oxford is that in a man's final

year he does not play cricket until he has sat Schools, which leaves him enough time to play in the last three county matches before the Varsity match. But as the new captain had no interest in graduating, he by-passed tradition and played cricket from the opening day of the summer season. His touch never failed him for he batted magnificently and on those rare occasions when he did have an off-day with the bat, he bowled superbly. During the term he led Oxford to victory over three county sides, and his team looked well set for their revenge in the Varsity match.

As the day of the match drew nearer, the cricket correspondent of *The Times* wrote that anyone who had seen him bat this season felt sure that the young Indian would follow his father into the record books by scoring a century against Cambridge; but the correspondent did add that he might be vulnerable against the early attack of Bill Potter, the Cambridge fast bowler.

Everyone wanted the Oxford captain to succeed, for he was one of those rare and gifted men whose charm creates no enemies.

When he announced his Blues team to the press, he did not send a telegram to his father for fear that the news might bring bad luck, and for good measure he did not speak to any member of the boat crew for the entire week leading up to the match. The night before the final encounter he retired to bed at seven, although he did not sleep.

* * *

On the first morning of the three-day match, the sun shone brightly in an almost cloudless sky and by eleven o'clock a fair-sized crowd were already in their seats. The two captains, in open-necked white shirts, spotless white pressed trousers and freshly creamed white boots, came out to study the pitch before they tossed. Robin Oakley of Cambridge won and elected to bat.

By lunch on the first day Cambridge had scored seventy-nine for three and in the early afternoon, when his fast bowlers were tired from their second spell and had not managed an early breakthrough, the captain put himself on. When he was straight, the ball didn't reach a full length, and when he bowled a full length, he was never straight; he quickly took himself off. His less established bowlers managed the necessary breakthrough and Cambridge were all out an hour after tea for 208.

The Oxford openers took the crease at ten past five; fifty minutes to see through before close of play on the first day. The captain sat padded up on the pavilion balcony, waiting to be called upon only if a wicket fell. His instructions had been clear: no heroics, bat out the forty minutes so that Oxford could start afresh the next morning with all ten wickets intact. With only one over left before the close of play, the young freshman opener had his middle stump removed by Bill Potter, the Cambridge fast bowler. Oxford were eleven for one. The captain came to the crease with only four balls left to face before the clock reached six. He took his usual guard, middle and leg, and prepared himself to face the fastest man in the Cambridge side. Potter's first delivery came rocketing down and was just short of a length, moving away outside the off stump. The ball nicked the edge of the bat — or was it pad? — and carried to first slip, who dived to his right and took the catch low down. Eleven Cambridge men screamed 'Howzat!' Was the captain going to be out — for a duck? Without waiting for the umpire's decision he turned and walked back to the pavilion, allowing no expression to appear on his face though he continually hit the side of his pad with his bat. As he climbed the steps he saw his father, sitting on his own in the members' enclosure. He walked on through the Long Room, to cries of 'Bad luck, old fellow' from men holding slopping pints of beer, and 'Better luck in the second innings' from large-bellied old Blues.

The next day, Oxford kept their heads down and put together a total of 181 runs, leaving themselves only a twenty-seven-run deficit. When Cambridge batted for a second time they pressed home their slight advantage and the captain's bowling figures ended up as eleven overs, no maidens, no wickets, forty-two runs. He took his team off the field at the end of play on the second day with Cambridge standing at 167 for seven, Robin Oakley the Cambridge captain having notched up a respectable sixty-three not out, and looking well set for a century.

On the morning of the third day, the Oxford quickies removed the last three Cambridge wickets for nineteen runs in forty minutes and Robin Oakley ran out of partners, and left the field with seventy-nine not out. The Oxford captain was the first to commiserate with him. 'At least you notched a hundred last year,' he added.

'True,' replied Oakley, 'so perhaps it's your turn this year. But not if I've got anything to do with it!'

The Oxford captain smiled at the thought of scoring a century when his team only needed 214 runs to win the match.

The two Oxford opening batsmen began their innings just before midday and remained together until the last over before lunch when the freshman was once again clean bowled by Cambridge's ace fast bowler, Bill Potter. The captain sat on the balcony nervously, padded up and ready. He looked down on the bald head of his father, who was chatting to a former captain of England. Both men had scored centuries in the Varsity match. The captain pulled on his gloves and walked slowly down the pavilion steps, trying to look casual; he had never felt more nervous in his life. As he passed his father, the older man turned his sun-burned face towards his only child and smiled. The crowd warmly applauded the captain all the way to the crease. He took guard, middle and leg again, and prepared to face the attack. The eager Potter who had despatched the captain so brusquely in the first innings came thundering down towards him hoping to be the cause of a pair. He delivered a magnificent first ball that swung into his legs and beat the captain all ends up, hitting him with a thud on the front pad.

'Howzat?' screamed Potter and the entire Cambridge side as they leaped in the air.

The captain looked up apprehensively at the umpire, who took his hands out of his pockets and moved a pebble from one palm to the other to remind him that another ball had been bowled. But he affected no interest in the appeal. A sigh of relief went up from the members in the pavilion. The captain managed to see through the rest of the over and returned to lunch nought not out, with his side twenty-four for one.

After lunch Potter returned to the attack. He rubbed the leather ball on his red-stained flannels and hurled himself forward, looking even fiercer than he had at start of play. He released his missile with every ounce of venom he possessed, but in so doing he tried a little too hard and the delivery was badly short. The captain leaned back and hooked the ball to the Tavern boundary for four, and from that moment he never looked as if anyone would prise him from the crease. He reached his fifty in seventy-one minutes, and at ten past four the Oxford team came into tea with the score at 171 for five and the skipper on eighty-two not out. The young man did not look at his father as he climbed the steps of the pavilion. He needed another eighteen runs before he could do that, and by then his team would be safe. He ate and drank nothing at tea, and spoke to no one.

After twenty minutes a bell rang and the eleven Cambridge men returned to the field. A minute later, the captain and his partner walked back out to the crease, their open white shirts flapping in the breeze. Two hours left for the century and victory. The captain's partner only lasted another five balls and the captain himself seemed to have lost that natural flow he had possessed before tea, struggling into the nineties with ones and twos. The light was getting bad and it took him a full thirty minutes to reach ninety-nine, by which time he had lost another partner: 194 for seven. He remained on ninety-nine for twelve minutes, when Robin Oakley the Cambridge captain took the new ball and brought his ace speed man back into the attack.

Then there occurred one of the most amazing incidents I have ever witnessed in a cricket match. Robin Oakley set an attacking field for the new ball — three slips, a gully, cover point, mid off, mid on, mid wicket and a short square leg, a truly vicious circle. He then tossed the ball to Potter who knew this would be his last chance to capture the Oxford captain's wicket and save the match; once he had scored the century he would surely knock off the rest of the runs in a matter of minutes. The sky was becoming bleak as a bank of dark clouds passed over the ground, but this was no time to leave the field for bad light. Potter shone the new ball once more on his white trousers and thundered up to hurl a delivery that the captain jabbed at and missed. One or two fielders raised their hands without appealing. Potter returned to his mark, shining the ball with even more relish, and left a red blood-like stain down the side of his thigh. The second ball, a yorker, beat the captain completely and must have missed the off stump by about an inch; there was a general sigh around the ground. The third ball hit the captain on the middle of the pad and the eleven Cambridge men threw their arms in the air and screamed for leg before wicket, but the umpire was not moved. The captain jabbed at the fourth ball and it carried tentatively to mid on, where Robin Oakley had placed himself a mere twenty yards in front of the bat, watching his adversary in disbelief as he set off for a run he could never hope to complete. His batting partner remained firmly in his crease, incredulous: one didn't run when the ball was hit to mid on unless it was the last delivery of the match.

The captain of Oxford, now stranded fifteen yards from safety, turned and looked at the captain of Cambridge, who held the ball in his hand. Robin Oakley was about to toss the ball to the wicket-keeper who in turn was waiting to remove the bails and send the Oxford captain back to the pavilion, run out for ninety-nine, but Oakley hesitated and, for several seconds the two gladiators stared at each other and then the Cambridge captain placed the ball in his pocket. The Oxford captain walked slowly back to his crease while the crowd remained silent in disbelief. Robin Oakley tossed the ball to Potter who thundered down to deliver the fifth ball, which was short, and the Oxford captain effortlessly placed it through the covers for four runs. The crowd rose as one and old friends in the pavilion thumped the father's back.

He smiled for a second time.

Potter was now advancing with his final effort and, exhausted, he delivered another short ball which should have been despatched to the boundary with ease, but the Oxford captain took one pace backwards and hit his own stumps. He was out, hit wicket, bowled Potter for 103. The crowd rose for a second time as he walked back to the pavilion and grown men who had been decorated in two wars had tears in their eyes. Seven minutes later, everyone left the field, drenched by a thunderstorm.

The match ended in a draw.

Just Good Friends

I woke up before him feeling slightly randy, but I knew there was nothing I could do about it.

I blinked and my eyes immediately accustomed themselves to the half-light. I raised my head and gazed at the large expanse of motionless white flesh lying next to me. If only he took as much exercise as I did he wouldn't have that spare tyre, I thought unsympathetically.

Roger stirred restlessly and even turned over to face me, but I knew he would not be fully awake until the alarm on his side of the bed started ringing. I pondered for a moment whether I could go back to sleep again or should get up and find myself some breakfast before he woke. In the end I settled for just lying still on my side day-dreaming, but making sure I didn't disturb him. When he did eventually open his eyes I planned to pretend I was still asleep — that way he would end up getting breakfast for me. I began to go over the things that needed to be done after he had left for the office. As long as I was at home ready to greet him when he returned from work, he didn't seem to mind what I got up to during the day.

A gentle rumble emanated from his side of the bed. Roger's snoring never disturbed me. My affection for him was unbounded, and I only wished I could find the words to let him know. In truth, he was the first man I had really appreciated. As I gazed at his unshaven face I was reminded that it hadn't been his looks which had attracted me in the pub that night.

I had first come across Roger in the Cat and Whistle, a public house situated on the corner of Mafeking Road. You might say it was our local. He used to come in around eight, order a pint of mild and take it to a small table in the corner of the room just beyond the dartboard. Mostly he would sit alone, watching the darts being thrown towards double top but more often settling in one or five, if they managed to land on the board at all. He never played the game himself, and I often wondered, from my vantage point behind the bar, if he was fearful of relinquishing his favourite seat or just had no interest in the sport.

Then things suddenly changed for Roger — for the better, was no doubt how he saw it — when one evening in early spring a blonde named Madeleine, wearing an imitation fur coat and drinking double gin and its, perched on the stool beside him. I had never seen her in the pub before but she was obviously known locally, and loose bar talk led me to believe it couldn't last. You see, word was about that she was looking for someone whose horizons stretched beyond the Cat and Whistle.

In fact the affair — if that's what it ever came to — lasted for only twenty days. I know because I counted every one of them. Then one night voices were raised and heads turned as she left the small stool just as suddenly as she had come. His tired eyes watched her walk to a vacant place at the corner of the bar, but he didn't show any surprise at her departure and made no attempt to pursue her.

Her exit was my cue to enter. I almost leapt from behind the bar and, moving as quickly as dignity allowed, was seconds later sitting on the vacant stool beside him. He didn't comment and certainly made no attempt to offer me a drink, but the one glance he shot in my direction did not suggest he found me an unacceptable replacement. I looked around to see if anyone else had plans to usurp my position. The men standing round the dartboard didn't seem to care. Treble seventeen, twelve and a five kept them more than occupied. I glanced towards the bar to check if the boss had noticed my absence, but he was busy taking orders. I saw Madeleine was already sipping a glass of champagne from the pub's only bottle, purchased by a stranger whose stylish double-breasted blazer and striped bow tie convinced me she wouldn't be bothering with Roger any longer. She looked well set for at least another twenty days.

I looked up at Roger — I had known his name for some time, although I had never addressed him as such and I couldn't be sure that he was aware of mine. I began to flutter my eyelashes in a rather exaggerated way. I felt a little stupid but at least it elicited a gentle smile. He leaned over and touched my cheek, his hands surprisingly gentle. Neither of us felt the need to speak. We were both lonely and it seemed unnecessary to explain why. We sat in silence, he occasionally sipping his beer, I from time to time rearranging my legs, while a few feet from us the darts pursued their undetermined course.

When the publican cried, 'Last orders,' Roger downed the remains of his beer while the dart players completed what had to be their final game.

No one commented when we left together, and I was surprised that Roger made no protest as I accompanied him back to his little semi-detached. I already knew exactly where he lived because I had seen him on several occasions standing at the bus queue in Dobson Street in a silent line of reluctant morning passengers. Once I even positioned myself on a nearby wall in order to study his features more carefully. It was an anonymous, almost common-place face, but he had the warmest eyes and the kindest smile I had observed in any man.

My only anxiety was that he didn't seem aware of my existence, just constantly preoccupied, his eyes each evening and his thoughts each morning only for Madeleine. How I envied that girl. She had everything I wanted — except a decent fur coat, the only thing my mother had left me. In truth, I have no right to be catty about Madeleine, as her past couldn't have been more murky than mine.

All that took place well over a year ago and, to prove my total devotion to Roger, I have never entered the Cat and Whistle since. He seemed to have forgotten Madeleine because he never once spoke of her in front of me. An unusual man, he didn't question me about any of my past relationships either.

Perhaps he should have. I would have liked

him to know the truth about my life before we'd met, though it all seems irrelevant now. You see, I had been the youngest in a family of four so I always came last in line. I had never known my father, and I arrived home one night to discover that my mother had run off with another man. Tracy, one of my sisters, warned me not to expect her back. She turned out to be right, for I have never seen my mother since that day. It's awful to have to admit, if only to oneself, that one's mother is a tramp.

Now an orphan, I began to drift, often trying to stay one step ahead of the law — not so easy when you haven't always got somewhere to put your head down. I can't even recall how I ended up with Derek — if that was his real name. Derek, whose dark sensual looks would have attracted any susceptible female, told me that he had been on a merchant steamer for the past three years. When he made love to me I was ready to believe anything. I explained to him that all I wanted was a warm home, regular food and perhaps in time a family of my own. He ensured that one of my wishes was fulfilled, because a few weeks after he left me I ended up with twins, two girls. Derek never set eyes on them: he had returned to sea even before I could tell him I was pregnant. He hadn't needed to promise me the earth; he was so good-looking he must have known I would have been his just for a night on the tiles.

I tried to bring up the girls decently, but the authorities caught up with me this time and I lost them both. I wonder where they are now?

God knows. I only hope they've ended up in a good home. At least they inherited Derek's irresistible looks, which can only help them through life. It's just one more thing Roger will never know about. His unquestioning trust only makes me feel more guilty, and now I never seem able to find a way of letting him know the truth.

After Derek had gone back to sea I was on my own for almost a year before getting part-time work at the Cat and Whistle. The publican was so mean that he wouldn't even have provided food and drink for me if I hadn't kept to my part of the bargain.

Roger used to come in about once, perhaps twice a week before he met the blonde with the shabby fur coat. After that it was every night until she upped and left him.

I knew he was perfect for me the first time I heard him order a pint of mild. A pint of mild — I can't think of a better description of Roger. In those early days the barmaids used to flirt openly with him, but he didn't show any interest. Until Madeleine latched on to him I wasn't even sure that it was women he preferred. Perhaps in the end it was my androgynous looks that appealed to him.

I think I must have been the only one in that pub who was looking for something more permanent.

And so Roger allowed me to spend the night with him. I remember that he slipped into the bathroom to undress while I rested on what I assumed would be my side of the bed. Since that night he has never once asked me to leave, let alone tried to kick me out. It's an easy-going relationship. I've never known him raise his voice or scold me unfairly. Forgive the cliché, but for once I have fallen on my feet.

Brr. Brr. Brr. That damned alarm. I wished I could have buried it. The noise would go on and on until at last Roger decided to stir himself. I once tried to stretch across him and put a stop to its infernal ringing, only ending up knocking the contraption on to the floor, which annoyed him even more than the ringing. Never again, I concluded. Eventually a long arm emerged from under the blanket and a palm dropped on to the top of the clock and the awful din subsided. I'm a light sleeper — the slightest movement stirs me. If only he had asked me I could have woken him far more gently each morning. After all, my methods are every bit as reliable as any man-made contraption.

Half awake, Roger gave me a brief cuddle before kneading my back, always guaranteed to elicit a smile. Then he yawned, stretched and declared as he did every morning, 'Must hurry along or I'll be late for the office.' I suppose some females would have been annoyed by the predictability of our morning routine — but not this lady. It was all part of a life that made me feel secure in the belief that at last I had found something worthwhile.

Roger managed to get his feet into the wrong slippers — always a fifty-fifty chance — before lumbering towards the bathroom. He emerged fifteen minutes later, as he always did, looking only slightly better than he had when he entered.

I've learned to live with what some would have called his foibles, while he has learned to accept my mania for cleanliness and a need to feel secure.

'Get up, lazy-bones,' he remonstrated, but then only smiled when I re-settled myself, refusing to leave the warm hollow that had been left by his body.

'I suppose you expect me to get your breakfast before I go to work?' he added as he made his way downstairs. I didn't bother to reply. I knew that in a few moments' time he would be opening the front door, picking up the morning newspaper, any mail, and our regular pint of milk. Reliable as ever, he would put on the kettle, then head for the pantry, fill a bowl with my favourite breakfast food and add my portion of the milk, leaving himself just enough for two cups of coffee.

I could anticipate almost to the second when breakfast would be ready. First I would hear the kettle boil, a few moments later the milk would be poured, then finally there would be the sound of a chair being pulled up. That was the signal I needed to confirm it was time for me to join him.

I stretched my legs slowly, noticing my nails needed some attention. I had already decided against a proper wash until after he had left for the office. I could hear the sound of the chair being scraped along the kitchen lino. I felt so happy that I literally jumped off the bed before making my way towards the open door. A few seconds later I was downstairs. Although he had already taken his first mouthful of cornflakes he stopped eating the moment he saw me.

'Good of you to join me,' he said, a grin spreading over his face.

I padded over towards him and looked up expectantly. He bent down and pushed my bowl towards me. I began to lap up the milk happily, my tail swishing from side to side.

It's a myth that we only swish our tails when we're angry.

Henry's Hiccup

When the grand Pasha's first son was born in 1900 (he had sired twelve daughters by six wives) he named the boy Henry, after his favourite king of England. Henry entered this world with more money than even the most blasé tax collector could imagine, and seemed destined to live a life of idle ease.

The Grand Pasha, who ruled over ten thousand families, was of the opinion that in time there would be only five kings left in the world — the kings of spades, hearts, diamonds, clubs, and England. With this conviction in mind, he decided that Henry should be educated by the British. The boy was therefore despatched from his native Cairo at the age of eight to embark upon a formal education, young enough to retain only vague recollections of the noise, the heat, and the dirt of his birthplace. Henry started his new life at the Dragon School, which the Grand Pasha's advisers assured him was the finest preparatory school in the land. The boy left this establishment four years later, having developed a passionate love for the polo field and a thorough distaste for the classroom. He proceeded, with the minimum academic qualifications, to Eton, which the Pasha's advisers assured him was the best school in Europe. He was gratified to learn the school had been founded by his favourite king. Henry spent five years at Eton, where he added squash, golf and tennis to his loves, and applied mathematics, jazz and cross-country running to his dislikes.

On leaving school, he once again failed to make more than a passing impression on the examiners. Nevertheless, he was found a place at Balliol College, Oxford, which the Pasha's advisers assured him was the greatest university in the world. Three years at Balliol added two more loves to his life: horses and women, and three more ineradicable aversions: politics, philosophy and economics.

At the end of his time *in statu pupillari*, he totally failed to impress the examiners and went down without a degree. His father, who considered young Henry's two goals against Cambridge in the Varsity polo match a wholly satisfactory result of his university career, despatched the boy on a journey round the world to complete his education. Henry enjoyed the experience, learning more on the racecourse at Longchamp and in the back streets of Benghazi than he had ever acquired from his formal upbringing in England.

The Grand Pasha would have been proud of the tall, sophisticated and handsome young man who returned to England a year later showing only the slightest trace of a foreign accent, if he hadn't died before his beloved son reached Southampton. Henry, although broken-hearted, was certainly not broke, as his father had left him some twenty million in known assets, including a racing stud in Suffolk, a 100-foot yacht at Nice, and a palace in Cairo. But by far the most important of his father's bequests was the finest manservant in London, one Godfrey Barker. Barker could arrange or rearrange anything, at a moment's notice.

Henry, for the lack of something better to do, settled himself into his father's old suite at the Ritz, not troubling to read the situations vacant column in *The Times*. Rather he embarked on a life of single-minded dedication to the pursuit of pleasure, the only career for which Eton, Oxford and inherited wealth had adequately equipped him. To do Henry justice, he had, despite a more than generous helping of charm and good looks, enough common sense to choose carefully those permitted to spend the unforgiving minute with him. He selected only old friends from school and university who, although they were without exception not as well-breeched as he, weren't the sort of fellows who came begging for the loan of a fiver to cover a gambling debt.

Whenever Henry was asked what was the first love of his life, he was always hard pressed to choose between horses and women, and as he found it possible to spend the day with the one and the night with the other without causing any jealousy or recrimination, he never overtaxed himself with resolving the problem. Most of his horses were fine stallions, fast, sleek, velvet-skinned, with dark eyes and firm limbs; this would have adequately described most of his women, except that they were fillies. Henry fell in and out of love with every girl in the chorus line of the London Palladium, and when the affairs had come to an end, Barker saw to it that they always received some suitable memento to ensure no scandal ensued. Henry also won every classic race on the English turf before he was thirty-five, and Barker always seemed to know the right year to back his master.

Henry's life quickly fell into a routine, never dull. One month was spent in Cairo going through the motions of attending to his business, three months in the south of France with the occasional excursion to Biarritz, and for the remaining eight months he resided at the Ritz. For the four months he was out of London his magnificent suite overlooking St James's Park remained unoccupied. History does not record whether Henry left the rooms empty because he disliked the thought of unknown persons splashing in the sunken marble bath, or because he simply couldn't be bothered with the fuss of signing in and out of the hotel twice a year. The Ritz management never commented on the matter to his father; why should they with the son? This programme fully accounted for Henry's year except for the odd trip to Paris when some home counties girl came a little too close to the altar. Although almost every girl who met Henry wanted to marry him, a good many would have done so even if he had been penniless. However, Henry saw absolutely no reason to be faithful to one woman. 'I have a hundred horses and a hundred male friends,' he would explain when asked. 'Why should I confine myself to one female?' There seemed no immediate answer to Henry's logic.

The story of Henry would have ended there

had he continued life as destiny seemed content to allow, but even the Henrys of this world have the occasional hiccup.

* * *

As the years passed, Henry grew into the habit of never planning ahead, as experience — and his able manservant, Barker — had always led him to believe that with vast wealth you could acquire anything you desired at the last minute, and cover any contingencies that arose later. However, even Barker couldn't formulate a contingency plan in response to Mr Chamberlain's statement of 3 September 1939 that the British people were at war with Germany. Henry felt it inconsiderate of Chamberlain to have declared war so soon after Wimbledon and the Oaks, and even more inconsiderate of the Home Office to advise him a few months later that Barker must stop serving the Grand Pasha and, until further notice, serve His Majesty the King instead.

What could poor Henry do? Now in his fortieth year, he was not used to living anywhere other than the Ritz, and the Germans who had caused Wimbledon to be cancelled were also occupying the George V in Paris and the Negresco in Nice. As the weeks passed and daily an invasion seemed more certain Henry came to the distasteful conclusion that he would have to return to a neutral Cairo until the British had won the war. It never crossed his mind, even for one moment, that the British might lose. After all, they had won the First World War, and therefore they must win the Second. 'History repeats itself' was about the only piece of wisdom he recalled clearly from three years of tutorials at Oxford.

Henry summoned the manager of the Ritz and told him that his suite was to be left unoccupied until he returned. He paid one year in advance, which he felt was more than enough time to take care of upstarts like Herr Hitler, and set off for Cairo. The manager was heard to remark later that the Grand Pasha's departure for Egypt was most ironic; he was, after all, more British than the British.

Henry spent a year at his palace in Cairo and then found he could bear his fellow countrymen no longer, so he removed himself to New York only just before it would have been possible for him to come face to face with Rommel. Once in New York, Henry bivouacked in the Pierre Hotel on Fifth Avenue, selected an American manservant called Eugene, and waited for Mr Churchill to finish the war. As if to prove his continuing support for the British, on the first of January every year he forwarded a cheque to the Ritz to cover the cost of his rooms for the next twelve months.

Henry celebrated VJ-Day in Times Square with a million Americans and immediately made plans for his return to Britain. He was surprised and disappointed when the British Embassy in Washington informed him that it might be some time before he was allowed to return to the land he loved, and despite continual pressure and all the influence he could bring to bear, he was unable to board a ship for Southampton until July 1946. From the first-class deck he waved goodbye to America and Eugene, and looked forward to England and Barker.

Once he had stepped off the ship on to English soil he headed straight for the Ritz to find his rooms exactly as he had left them. As far as Henry could see, nothing had changed except that his manservant (now the batman to a general) could not be released from the armed forces for at least another six months. Henry was determined to play his part in the war effort by surviving without him for that period, and remembering Barker's words: 'Everyone knows who you are. Nothing will change,' he felt confident all would be well. Indeed, on the *Bonheur-du-jour* in his room at the Ritz was an invitation to dine with Lord and Lady Lympsham in their Chelsea Square home the following night. It looked as if Barker's prediction was turning out to be right: everything would be just the same. Henry penned an affirmative reply to the invitation, happy with the thought that he was going to pick up his life in England exactly where he had left off.

The following evening Henry arrived on the Chelsea Square doorstep a few minutes after eight o'clock. The Lympshams, an elderly couple who had not qualified for the war in any way, gave every appearance of not even realising that it had taken place, or that Henry had been absent from the London social scene. Their table, despite rationing, was as fine as Henry remembered and, more important, one of the guests present was quite unlike anyone he could ever remember. Her name, Henry learned from his host, was Victoria Campbell, and she turned out to be the daughter of another guest, General Sir Ralph Colquhoun. Lady Lympsham confided to Henry over the quails' eggs that the sad young thing had lost her husband when the Allies advanced on Berlin, only a few days before the Germans had surrendered. For the first time Henry felt guilty about not having played some part in the war.

All through dinner, he could not take his eyes from young Victoria, whose classical beauty was only equalled by her well-informed and lively conversation. He feared he might be staring too obviously at the slim, dark-haired girl with the high cheek-bones; it was like admiring a beautiful sculpture and wanting to touch it. Her bewitching smile elicited an answering smile from all who received it. Henry did everything in his power to be the receiver and was rewarded on several occasions, aware that, for the first time in his life, he was becoming totally infatuated — and was delighted to be.

The ensuing courtship was an unusual one for Henry, in that he made no attempt to persuade Victoria to compliance. He was sympathetic and attentive, and when she had come out of mourning he approached her father and asked if he might request his daughter's hand in marriage. Henry was overjoyed when first the General agreed and later Victoria accepted. After an announcement in *The Times* they celebrated the engagement with a small dinner party at the Ritz, attended by one hundred and twenty close friends who might have been forgiven for coming to the conclusion that Attlee was exaggerating about his austerity programme. After the last guest had left Henry walked Victoria back to her father's home in Belgrave Mews, while discussing the wedding arrangements and his plans for the honeymoon.

'Everything must be perfect for you, my angel,' he said, as once again he admired the way her long, dark hair curled at the shoulders. 'We shall be married in St Margaret's, Westminster, and after a reception at the Ritz we will be driven to Victoria Station where you will be met by Fred, the senior porter. Fred will allow no one else to carry my bags to the last carriage of the Golden Arrow. One should always have the last carriage, my darling,' explained Henry, 'so that one cannot be disturbed by other travellers.'

Victoria was impressed by Henry's mastery of the arrangements, especially remembering the absence of his manservant, Barker.

Henry warmed to his theme. 'Once we have boarded the Golden Arrow, you will be served with China tea and some wafer-thin smoked salmon sandwiches which we can enjoy while relaxing on our journey to Dover. When we arrive at the Channel port, you will be met by Albert, whom Fred will have alerted. Albert will remove the bags from our carriage, but not before everyone else has left the train. He will then escort us to the ship, where we will take sherry with the captain while our bags are being placed in Cabin Number Three. Like my father, I always have Cabin Number Three; it is not only the largest and most comfortable stateroom on board, but it is situated in the centre of the ship, which makes it possible to enjoy a comfortable crossing even should one have the misfortune to encounter bad weather. And when we have docked in Calais you will find Pierre waiting for us. He will have organised everything for the front carriage of the Flèche d'Or.'

'Such a programme must take a considerable amount of detailed planning,' said Victoria, her hazel eyes sparkling as she listened to her future husband's description of the promised tour.

'More tradition than organisation I would say, my dear,' replied Henry, smiling, as they strolled hand in hand across Hyde Park. 'Although, I confess, in the past Barker has kept his eye on things should any untoward emergency arise. In any case, I have *always* had the front carriage of the Flèche d'Or, because it assures one of being off the train and away before anyone realises that you have actually arrived in Paris. Other than Raymond, of course.'

'Raymond?'

'Yes, Raymond, a servant *par excellence*, who adored my father, he will have organised a bottle of Veuve Clicquot '37 and a little Russian caviar for the journey. He will also have ensured that there is a couch in the railway carriage should you need to rest, my dear.'

'You seem to have thought of everything,

Henry darling,' she said as they entered Belgrave Mews.

'I hope you will think so, Victoria; for when you arrive in Paris, which I have not had the opportunity to visit for so many years, there will be a Rolls-Royce standing by the side of the carriage, door open, and you will step out of the Flèche d'Or into the car and Maurice will drive us to the George V, arguably the finest hotel in Europe. Louis, the manager, will be on the steps of the hotel to greet you and he will conduct us to the bridal suite with its stunning view of the city. A maid will unpack for you while you retire to bathe and rest from the tiresome journey. When you are fully recovered we shall dine at Maxim's, where you will be guided to the corner table furthest from the orchestra by Marcel, the finest head waiter in the world. As you are seated, the musicians will strike up 'A Room with a View', my favourite tune, and we will then be served with the most magnificent langouste you have ever tasted, of that I can assure you.'

Henry and Victoria arrived at the front door of the General's small house in Belgrave Mews. He took her hand before continuing.

'After you have dined, my dear, we shall stroll into the Madeleine, where I shall buy a dozen red roses from Paulette, the most beautiful flower girl in Paris. She is almost as lovely as you.' Henry sighed and concluded: 'Then we shall return to the George V and spend our first night together.'

Victoria's hazel eyes showed delighted anticipation.

'I only wish it could be tomorrow,' she said.

Henry kissed her gallantly on the cheek and said: 'It will be worth waiting for, my dear, I can assure you it will be a day neither of us will ever forget.'

'I'm sure of that,' Victoria replied as he released her hand.

* * *

On the morning of his wedding Henry leaped out of bed and drew back the curtains with a flourish, only to be greeted by a steady drizzle.

'The rain will clear by eleven o'clock,' he said out loud with immense confidence, and hummed as he shaved slowly and with care.

The weather had not improved by mid-morning. On the contrary, heavy rain was falling by the time Victoria entered the church. Henry's disappointment evaporated the instant he saw his beautiful bride; all he could think of was taking her to Paris. The ceremony over, the Grand Pasha and his wife stood outside the church, a golden couple, smiling for the press photographers as the loyal guests scattered damp rice over them. As soon as they decently could, they set off for the reception at the Ritz. Between them they managed to chat to every guest, and they would have been away in better time had Victoria been a little quicker changing and the General's toast to the happy couple been considerably shorter. The guests crowded on to the steps of the Ritz, overflowing on to the pavement in Piccadilly to wave goodbye to the departing honeymooners, and were sheltered from the downpour by a capacious red awning.

The General's Rolls took the Grand Pasha and his wife to the station, where the chauffeur unloaded the bags. Henry instructed him to return to the Ritz, as he had everything under control. The chauffeur touched his cap and said: 'I hope you and madam have a wonderful trip, sir,' and left them. Henry stood on the station, looking for Fred. There was no sign of him, so he hailed a passing porter.

'Where is Fred?' enquired Henry.

'Fred who?' came the reply.

'How in heaven's name should I know?' said Henry.

'Then how in hell's name should I know?' retorted the porter.

Victoria shivered. English railway stations are not designed for the latest fashion in silk coats.

'Kindly take my bags to the end carriage of the train,' said Henry.

The porter looked down at the fourteen bags. 'All right,' he said reluctantly.

Henry and Victoria stood patiently in the cold as the porter loaded the bags on to his trolley and trundled them off along the platform.

'Don't worry, my dear,' said Henry. 'A cup of Lapsang Souchong tea and some smoked salmon sandwiches and you'll feel a new girl.'

'I'm just fine,' said Victoria, smiling, though not quite as bewitchingly as normal, as she put her arm through her husband's. They strolled along together to the end carriage.

'Can I check your tickets, sir?' said the

conductor, blocking the entrance to the last carriage.

'My what?' said Henry, his accent sounding unusually pronounced.

'Your tic . . . kets,' said the conductor, conscious he was addressing a foreigner.

'In the past I have always made the arrangements on the train, my good man.'

'Not nowadays you don't, sir. You'll have to go to the booking office and buy your tickets like everyone else, and you'd better be quick about it, because the train is due to leave in a few minutes.'

Henry stared at the conductor in disbelief. 'I assume my wife may rest on the train while I go and purchase the tickets,' he said.

'No, I'm sorry, sir. No one is allowed to board the train unless they are in possession of a valid ticket.'

'Remain here, my dear,' said Henry, 'and I will deal with this little problem immediately. Kindly direct me to the ticket office, porter.'

'End of Platform Four, governor,' said the conductor, slamming the train door, annoyed at being described as a porter.

That wasn't quite what Henry had meant by 'direct me'. Nevertheless, he left his bride with the fourteen bags and somewhat reluctantly headed back towards the ticket office at the end of Platform Four, where he went to the front of a long line.

'There's a queue, you know, mate,' someone shouted.

Henry didn't know. 'I'm in a frightful hurry,' he said.

'And so am I,' came back the reply, 'so get to the back.'

Henry had been told that the British were good at standing in queues, but as he had never had to join one before that moment, he was quite unable to confirm or deny the rumour. He reluctantly walked to the back of the queue. It took some time before he reached the front.

'I would like to take the last carriage to Dover.'

'You would like what . . . ?'

'The last carriage,' repeated Henry a little more loudly.

'I'm sorry, sir, but every first-class seat is sold.'

'I don't want a seat,' said Henry. 'I require the carriage.'

'There are no carriages available nowadays, sir, and as I said, all the seats in first class are sold. I can still fix you up in third class.'

'I don't mind what it costs,' said Henry. 'I must travel first class.'

'I don't have a first-class seat, sir. It wouldn't matter if you could afford the whole train.'

'I can,' said Henry.

'I still don't have a seat left in first class,' said the clerk unhelpfully.

Henry would have persisted, but several people in the queue behind him were pointing out that there were only two minutes before the train was due to leave, and that they wanted to catch it even if he didn't.

'Two seats then,' said Henry, unable to make himself utter the words 'third class'.

Two green tickets marked 'Dover' were handed through the little grille. Henry took them and started to walk away.

'That will be seventeen and sixpence please, sir.'

'Oh, yes, of course,' said Henry apologetically. He fumbled in his pocket and unfolded one of the three large white five-pound notes he always carried on him.

'Don't you have anything smaller?'

'No, I do not,' said Henry, who found the idea of carrying money vulgar enough without it having to be in small denominations.

The clerk handed back four pounds and a half-crown. Henry did not pick up the half-crown.

'Thank you, sir,' said the startled man. It was more than his Saturday bonus.

Henry put the tickets in his pocket and quickly returned to Victoria, who was smiling defiantly against the cold wind; it was not quite the smile that had originally captivated him. Their porter had long ago disappeared, and Henry couldn't see another in sight. The conductor took his tickets and clipped them.

'All aboard,' he shouted, waved a green flag and blew his whistle.

Henry quickly threw all fourteen bags through the open door and pushed Victoria on to the moving train before leaping on himself. Once he had caught his breath he walked down the corridor, staring into the third-class carriages. He had never seen one before. The seats were nothing more than thin worn-out cushions, and as he looked into one half-full carriage a young couple jumped in and took the last two adjacent seats. Henry searched frantically for a free carriage but he was unable even to find one with two seats together. Victoria took a single seat in a packed compartment without complaint, while Henry sat forlornly on one of the suitcases in the corridor.

'It will be different once we're in Dover,' he said, without his usual self-confidence.

'I am sure it will be, Henry,' she replied, smiling kindly at him.

The two-hour journey seemed interminable. Passengers of all shapes and sizes squeezed past Henry in the corridor, treading on his Lobbs hand-made leather shoes with the words:

'Sorry, sir.'

'Sorry, guv.'

'Sorry, mate.'

Henry put the blame firmly on the shoulders of Clement Attlee and his ridiculous campaign for social equality, and waited for the train to reach Dover Priory Station. The moment the engine pulled in Henry leaped out of the carriage first, not last, and called for Albert at the top of his voice. Nothing happened, except that a stampede of people rushed past him on their way to the ship. Eventually Henry spotted a porter and rushed over to him, only to find he was already loading up his trolley with someone else's luggage. Henry sprinted to a second man and then on to a third, and waved a pound note at a fourth, who came immediately and unloaded the fourteen bags.

'Where to, guv?' asked the porter amicably.

'The ship,' said Henry, and returned to claim

his bride. He helped Victoria down from the train and they both ran through the rain until, breathless, they reached the gangplank of the ship.

'Tickets, sir,' said a young officer in a dark blue uniform at the bottom of the gangplank.

'I always have Cabin Number Three,' said Henry between breaths.

'Of course, sir,' said the young man, and looked at his clipboard. Henry smiled confidently at Victoria.

'Mr and Mrs William West.'

'I beg your pardon?' said Henry.

'You must be Mr William West.'

'I certainly am not. I am the Grand Pasha of Cairo.'

'Well, I'm sorry, sir, Cabin Number Three is booked in the name of a Mr William West and family.'

'I have never been treated by Captain Rogers in this cavalier fashion before,' said Henry, his accent now even more pronounced. 'Send for him immediately.'

'Captain Rogers was killed in the war, sir. Captain Jenkins is now in command of this ship, and he never leaves the bridge thirty minutes before sailing.'

Henry's exasperation was turning to panic. 'Do you have a free cabin?'

The young officer looked down his list. 'No, sir, I'm afraid not. The last one was taken a few minutes ago.'

'May I have two tickets?' asked Henry.

'Yes, sir,' said the young officer. 'But you'll

have to buy them from the booking office on the quayside.'

Henry decided that any further argument would be only time-consuming, so he turned on his heel without another word, leaving his wife with the laden porter. He strode to the booking office.

'Two first-class tickets to Calais,' he said firmly.

The man behind the little glass pane gave Henry a tired look. 'It's all one class nowadays, sir, unless you have a cabin.' He proffered two tickets. 'That will be one pound exactly.'

Henry handed over a pound note, took his tickets, and hurried back to the young officer.

The porter was offloading their suitcases on to the quayside.

'Can't you take them on board,' cried Henry, 'and put them in the hold?'

'No, sir, not now. Only the passengers are allowed on board after the ten-minute signal.'

Victoria carried two of the smaller suitcases, and Henry humped the twelve remaining ones in relays up the gangplank. He finally sat down on the deck exhausted. Every seat seemed already to be occupied. Henry couldn't make up his mind if he was cold from the rain or hot from his exertions. Victoria's smile was fixed firmly in place as she took his hand.

'Don't worry about a thing, darling,' she said. 'Just relax and enjoy the crossing; it will be such fun being out on deck together.'

The ship moved sedately out of the calm of the harbour into the Dover Straits. Later that night Captain Jenkins told his wife that the twenty-five-mile journey had been among the most unpleasant crossings he had ever experienced. He added that he had nearly turned back when his second officer, a veteran of two wars, was violently sick. Henry and Victoria spent most of the trip hanging over the rails getting rid of everything they had consumed at their reception. Two people had never been more happy to see land in their life than they were at the first sight of the Normandy coastline. They staggered off the ship, taking the suitcases one at a time.

'Perhaps France will be different,' Henry said lamely, and after a perfunctory search for Pierre he went straight to the booking office and obtained two third-class seats on the Flèche d'Or. They were at least able to sit next to each other this time, but in a carriage already occupied by six other passengers, as well as a dog and a hen. The six of them left Henry in no doubt that they enjoyed the modern habit of smoking in public and the ancient custom of taking garlic in their food. He would have been sick again at any other time, but there was nothing left in his stomach. He considered walking up and down the train searching for Raymond, but feared it would only result in him losing his seat next to Victoria. He gave up trying to hold any conversation with her above the noise of the dog, the hen and the Gallic babble, and satisfied himself with looking out of the window, watching the French countryside and, for the first time in his life, noting the name of every station through which they passed.

Once they arrived at the Gare du Nord Henry made no attempt to look for Maurice, but simply headed straight for the nearest taxi rank. By the time he had transferred all fourteen cases he was well down the queue. He and Victoria stood there for just over an hour, moving the cases forward inch by inch until it was their turn.

'*Monsieur*?'

'Do you speak English?'

'*Un peu, un peu*.'

'Hotel George V.'

'*Oui, mais je ne peux pas mettre toutes les valises dans le coffre*.'

So Henry and Victoria sat huddled in the back of the taxi, bruised, tired, soaked and starving, surrounded by leather suitcases, only to be bumped up and down over the cobbled stones all the way to the George V.

The hotel doorman rushed to help them as Henry offered the taxi driver a pound note.

'No take English money, monsieur.'

Henry couldn't believe his ears. The doorman happily paid the taxi driver in francs, and quickly pocketed the pound note. Henry was too tired even to comment. He helped Victoria up the marble steps and went over to the reception desk.

'The Grand Pasha of Cairo and his wife. The bridal suite, please.'

'*Oui, monsieur*.'

Henry smiled at Victoria.

'You 'ave your booking confirmation with you?'

'No,' said Henry. 'I have never needed to confirm my booking with you in the past. Before the war I . . .'

'I am sorry, sir, but the 'otel is fully booked at the moment. A conference.'

'Even the bridal suite?' asked Victoria.

'Yes, madam, the chairman and his lady, you understand.' He nearly winked.

Henry certainly did not understand. There had always been a room for him at the George V whenever he had wanted one in the past. Desperate, he unfolded the second of his five-pound notes and slipped it across the counter.

'Ah,' said the booking clerk, 'I see we still have one room unoccupied, but I fear it is not very large.'

Henry waved a listless hand.

The booking clerk banged the bell on the counter in front of him with the palm of his hand, and a porter appeared immediately and escorted them to the promised room. The booking clerk had been telling the truth. Henry could only have described what they found themselves standing in as a box room. The reason that the curtains were perpetually drawn was that the view, over the chimneys of Paris, was singularly unprepossessing, but that was not to be the final blow, as Henry realised, staring in disbelief at the two narrow single beds. Victoria started unpacking without a word while Henry slumped despondently on the end of one of them. After Victoria had sat soaking in a bath that was the perfect size for a six-year-old, she lay down exhausted on the other bed. Neither spoke for nearly an hour.

'Come on, darling,' said Henry finally. 'Let's go and have dinner.'

Victoria rose loyally but reluctantly and dressed for dinner while Henry sat in the bath, knees on nose, trying to wash himself before changing into evening dress. This time he phoned the front desk and ordered a taxi as well as booking a table at Maxim's.

The taxi driver did accept his pound note on this occasion, but as Henry and his bride entered the great restaurant he recognised no one and no one recognised him. A waiter led them to a small table hemmed in between two other couples just below the band. As he walked into the dining room the musicians struck up 'Alexander's Ragtime Band'.

They ordered from the extensive menu, and the langouste turned out to be excellent, every bit as good as Henry had promised, but by then neither of them had the stomach to eat a full meal and the greater part of both their dishes was left on the plate.

Henry found it hard to convince the new head waiter that the lobster had been superb and that they had not purposely come to Maxim's not to eat it. Over coffee, he took Victoria's hand and tried to apologise.

'Let us end this farce,' he said, 'by completing my plan and going to the Madeleine and presenting you with the promised flowers. Paulette will not be in the square to greet you, but there will surely be someone who can sell us roses.'

Henry called for the bill and unfolded the third five-pound note (Maxim's are always happy to accept other people's currency, and certainly didn't bother him with any change). They left, walking hand in hand towards the Madeleine. For once Henry turned out to be right, for Paulette was nowhere to be seen. An old woman with a shawl over her head and a wart on the side of her nose stood in her place on the corner of the square, surrounded by the most beautiful flowers.

Henry selected a dozen of the longest-stemmed red roses and placed them in the arms of his bride. The old woman smiled at Victoria.

Victoria returned her smile.

'*Dix francs, monsieur,*' said the old woman to Henry.

Henry fumbled in his pocket, only to discover he had spent all his money. He looked despairingly at the old woman, who raised her hands, smiled at him, and said:

'Don't worry, Henry, have them on me. For old times' sake.'

A Matter Of Principle

Sir Hamish Graham had many of the qualities and most of the failings that result from being born to a middle-class Scottish family. He was well educated, hardworking and honest, while at the same time being narrow-minded, uncompromising and proud. Never on any occasion had he allowed hard liquor to pass his lips, and he mistrusted all men who had not been born north of Hadrian's Wall, and many of those who had.

After spending his formative years at Fettes School, to which he had won a minor scholarship, and at Edinburgh University, where he obtained a second-class honours degree in engineering, he was chosen from a field of twelve to be a trainee with the international construction company TarMac (named after its founder, J. L. McAdam, who discovered that tar when mixed with stones was the best constituent for making roads). The new trainee, through diligent work and uncompromising tactics, became the firm's youngest and most disliked project manager. By the age of thirty Graham had been appointed deputy managing director of TarMac and was already beginning to realise that he could not hope to progress much farther while he was in someone else's employ. He therefore started to consider forming his own company. When two years later the chairman of TarMac, Sir Alfred Hickman, offered Graham the opportunity to replace the retiring managing director, he resigned immediately. After all, if Sir Alfred felt he had the ability to run TarMac, he must be competent enough to start his own company.

The next day, young Hamish Graham made an appointment to see the local manager of the Bank of Scotland who was responsible for the TarMac account, and with whom he had dealt for the past ten years. Graham explained to the manager his plans for the future, submitting a full written proposal, and requesting that his overdraft facility might be extended from fifty pounds to ten thousand. Three weeks later he learned that his application had been viewed favourably. He remained in his lodgings in Edinburgh, while renting an office (or, to be more accurate, a room) in the north of the city at ten shillings a week. He purchased a typewriter, hired a secretary and ordered some unembossed headed letter-paper. After a further month of diligent interviewing, he employed two engineers, both graduates of Aberdeen University, and five out-of-work labourers from Glasgow.

During those first few weeks on his own Graham tendered for several small road contracts in the central lowlands of Scotland, the first seven of which he failed to secure. Preparing a tender is always tricky and often expensive, so by the end of his first six months in business Graham was beginning to wonder if his sudden departure from TarMac had not been foolhardy. For the first time in his life he experienced self-doubt, but that was soon removed by the

Ayrshire County Council, who accepted his tender to construct a minor road which was to join a projected school to the main highway. The road was only five hundred yards in length, but the assignment took Graham's little team seven months to complete, and when all the bills had been paid and all expenses taken into account Graham Construction made a net loss of £143.10s.6d.

Still, in the profit column was a small reputation which had been invisibly earned, and which caused the Ayrshire Council to invite him to build the school at the end of the new road. This contract made Graham Construction a profit of £420 and added still further to his reputation. From that moment Graham Construction went from strength to strength, and as early as his third year in business Graham was able to declare a small pre-tax profit, and this grew steadily over the next five years. When Graham Construction was floated on the London Stock Exchange the demand for the shares was over-subscribed ten times and the newly quoted company was soon considered a blue-chip institution, a considerable achievement for Graham to have pulled off in his own lifetime. But then, the City likes men who grow slowly and can be relied on not to involve themselves in unnecessary risks.

In the sixties Graham Construction built motorways, hospitals, factories, and even a power station, but the achievement the chairman took most pride in was Edinburgh's newly completed art gallery, which was the only contract that showed a deficit in the annual general report. The invisible earnings column, however, recorded the award of knight bachelor for the chairman.

Sir Hamish decided that the time had come for Graham Construction to expand into new fields, and looked, as generations of Scots had before him, towards the natural market of the British Empire. He built in Australia and Canada with his own finances, and in India and Africa with a subsidy from the British government. In 1963 he was named 'Businessman of the Year' by *The Times* and three years later 'Chairman of the Year' by *The Economist*. Sir Hamish never once altered his methods to keep pace with the changing times, and if anything grew more stubborn in the belief that his ideas of doing business were correct whatever anyone else thought; and he had a long credit column to prove he was right.

In the early seventies, when the slump hit the construction business, Graham Construction suffered the same cut in budgets and lost contracts as its major competitors. Sir Hamish reacted in a predictable way, by tightening his belt and paring his estimates while at the same time refusing to compromise his business principles one jot. The company therefore grew leaner and many of his more enterprising young executives left Graham Construction for firms which still believed in taking on the occasional risky contract.

Only when the slope of the profits graph started taking on the look of a downhill slalom did Sir Hamish become worried. One night, while brooding over the company's profit-and-loss account for the previous three years, and realising that he was losing contracts even in his native Scotland, Sir Hamish reluctantly came to the conclusion that he must tender for less established work, and perhaps even consider the odd gamble.

His brightest young executive, David Heath, a stocky, middle-aged bachelor, whom he did not entirely trust — after all, the man had been educated south of the border and worse, some extraordinary place in the United States called the Wharton Business School — wanted Sir Hamish to put a toe into Mexican waters. Mexico, as Heath was not slow to point out, had discovered vast reserves of oil off their eastern coast and had overnight become rich with American dollars. The construction business in Mexico was suddenly proving most lucrative and contracts were coming up for tender with figures as high as thirty to forty million dollars attached to them. Heath urged Sir Hamish to go after one such contract that had recently been announced in a full-page advertisement in *The Economist*. The Mexican government were issuing tender documents for a proposed ring road around their capital, Mexico City. In an article in the business section of the *Observer*, detailed arguments were put forward as to why established British companies should try to fulfil the ring-road tender. Heath had offered shrewd advice on overseas contracts in the past that Sir Hamish had let slip through his fingers.

The next morning, Sir Hamish sat at his desk listening attentively to David Heath, who felt that as Graham Construction had already built the Glasgow and Edinburgh ring roads, any application they made to the Mexican government had to be taken seriously. To Heath's surprise, Sir Hamish agreed with his project manager and allowed a team of six men to travel to Mexico to obtain the tender documents and research the project.

The research team was led by David Heath, and consisted of three other engineers, a geologist and an accountant. When the team arrived in Mexico they obtained the tender documents from the Minister of Works and settled down to study them minutely. Having pinpointed the major problems they walked around Mexico City with their ears open and their mouths shut and made a list of the problems they were clearly going to encounter: the impossibility of unloading anything at Vera Cruz and then transporting the cargo to Mexico City without half of the original consignment being stolen, the lack of communications between ministries, and worst of all the attitude of the Mexicans to work. But David Heath's most positive contribution to the list was the discovery that each minister had his own outside man, and that man had better be well disposed to Graham Construction if the firm were to be even considered for the shortlist. Heath immediately sought out the Minister of Works' man, one Victor Perez, and took him to an extravagant lunch at the *Fonda el Refugio* where both of them nearly ended up drunk, although Heath remained sober enough to agree all of the necessary terms, conditional upon Sir Hamish's approval. Having taken every possible precaution, Heath agreed on a tender figure with Perez which was to include the minister's percentage. Once he had completed the report for his chairman, he flew back to England with his team.

On the evening of David Heath's return, Sir Hamish retired to bed early to study his project manager's conclusions. He read the report through the night as others might read a spy story, and was left in no doubt that this was the opportunity he had been looking for to overcome the temporary setbacks Graham Construction was now suffering. Although Sir Hamish would be up against Costains, Sunleys and John Brown, as well as many international companies, he still felt confident that any application he made must have a 'fair chance'. On arrival at his office the next morning Sir Hamish sent for David Heath, who was delighted by the chairman's initial response to his report.

Sir Hamish started speaking as soon as his burly project manager entered the room, not even inviting him to take a seat.

'You must contact our Embassy in Mexico City immediately and inform them of our intentions,' pronounced Sir Hamish. 'I may speak to the Ambassador myself,' he said, intending that to be the concluding remark of the interview.

'Useless,' said David Heath.

'I beg your pardon?'

'I don't wish to appear rude, sir, but it doesn't work like that any more. Britain is no longer a great power dispensing largesse to all far-flung and grateful recipients.'

'More's the pity,' said Sir Hamish.

The project manager continued as though he had not heard the remark.

'The Mexicans now have vast wealth of their own, and the United States, Japan, France and Germany keep massive embassies in Mexico City with highly professional trade delegations trying to influence every ministry.'

'But surely history counts for something,' said Sir Hamish. 'Wouldn't they rather deal with an established British company than some upstarts from — ?'

'Perhaps, sir, but in the end all that really matters is which minister is in charge of what contract and who is his outside representative.'

Sir Hamish looked puzzled. 'Your meaning is obscure to me, Mr Heath.'

'Allow me to explain, sir. Under the present system in Mexico, each ministry has an allocation of money to spend on projects agreed to by the government. Every Secretary of State is acutely aware that his tenure of office may be very short, so he picks out a major contract for himself from the many available. It's the one way to ensure a pension for life if the government is changed overnight or the minister simply loses his job.'

'Don't bandy words with me, Mr Heath. What you are suggesting is that I should bribe a government official. I have never been involved in that sort of thing in thirty years of business.'

'And I wouldn't want you to start now,' replied Heath. 'The Mexican is far too experienced in business etiquette for anything as clumsy as that to be suggested, but while the law requires that you appoint a Mexican agent, it must make sense to try and sign up the minister's man, who in the end is the one person who can ensure that you will be awarded the contract. The system seems to work well, and as long as a minister deals only with reputable international firms and doesn't become greedy, no one complains. Fail to observe either of those two golden rules and the whole house of cards collapses. The minister ends up in Le Cumberri for thirty years and the company concerned has all its assets expropriated and is banned from any future business dealings in Mexico.'

'I really cannot become involved in such shenanigans,' said Sir Hamish. 'I still have my shareholders to consider.'

'*You* don't have to become involved,' Heath rejoined. 'After we have tendered for the contract you wait and see if the company has been shortlisted and then, if we have, you wait again to find out if the minister's man approaches us. I know the man, so if he does make contact we have a deal. After all, Graham Construction is a respectable international company.'

'Precisely, and that's why it's against my principles,' said Sir Hamish with hauteur.

'I do hope, Sir Hamish, it's also against your principles to allow the Germans and the

Americans to steal the contract from under our noses.'

Sir Hamish glared back at his project manager but remained silent.

'And I feel I must add, sir,' said David Heath, moving restlessly from foot to foot, 'that the pickings in Scotland haven't exactly yielded a harvest lately.'

'All right, all right, go ahead,' said Sir Hamish reluctantly. 'Put in a tender figure for the Mexico City ring road, but be warned, if I find bribery is involved, on your head be it,' he added, banging his fist on the table.

'What tender figure have you settled on, sir?' asked the project manager. 'I believe, as I stressed in my report, that we should keep the amount under forty million dollars.'

'Agreed,' said Sir Hamish, who paused for a moment and smiled to himself before saying: 'Make it $39,121,110.'

'Why that particular figure, sir?'

'Sentimental reasons,' said Sir Hamish, without further explanation.

David Heath left, pleased that he had convinced his boss to go ahead, although he feared it might in the end prove harder to overcome Sir Hamish's principles than the entire Mexican government. Nevertheless he filled in the bottom line of the tender as instructed and then had the document signed by three directors including his chairman, as required by Mexican law. He sent the tender by special messenger to the Ministry of Buildings in Paseo de la Reforma: when tendering for a contract for over thirty-nine million dollars, one does not send the document by first-class post.

Several weeks passed before the Mexican Embassy in London contacted Sir Hamish, requesting that he travel to Mexico City for a meeting with Manuel Unichurtu, the minister concerned with the city's ring-road project. Sir Hamish remained sceptical, but David Heath was jubilant, because he had already learned through another source that Graham Construction was the only tender being seriously considered at that moment, although there were one or two outstanding items still to be agreed on. David Heath knew exactly what that meant.

A week later Sir Hamish, travelling first class, and David Heath, travelling economy, flew out of Heathrow bound for Mexico International Airport. On arrival they took an hour to clear customs and another thirty minutes to find a taxi to take them to the city, and then only after the driver had bargained with them for an outrageous fare. They covered the fifteen-mile journey from the airport to their hotel in just over an hour, and Sir Hamish was able to observe at first hand why the Mexicans were so desperate to build a ring road. Even with the windows down the ten-year-old car was like an oven that had been left on high all night, but during the journey Sir Hamish never once loosened his collar or tie. The two men checked into their rooms, phoned the minister's secretary to inform her of their arrival, and then waited.

For two days, nothing happened.

David Heath assured his chairman that such a

hold-up was not an unusual course of events in Mexico, as the minister was undoubtedly in meetings most of the day, and after all, wasn't '*mañana*' the one Spanish word every foreigner understood?

On the afternoon of the third day, just as Sir Hamish was threatening to return home, David Heath received a call from the minister's man, who accepted an invitation to join them both for dinner in Sir Hamish's suite that evening.

Sir Hamish put on evening dress for the occasion, despite David Heath's counselling against the idea. He even had a bottle of *Fina La Ina* sherry sent up in case the minister's man required some refreshment. The dinner table was set and the hosts were ready for seven-thirty. The minister's man did not appear at seven-thirty, or seven-forty-five, or eight o'clock, or eight-fifteen, or eight-thirty. At eight-forty-nine there was a loud rap on the door, and Sir Hamish muttered an inaudible reproach as David Heath went to open it. He found his contact standing there.

'Good evening, Mr Heath. I'm sorry to be late. Held up with the minister, you understand.'

'Yes, of course,' said David Heath. 'How good of you to come, Señor Perez. May I introduce my chairman, Sir Hamish Graham?'

'How do you do, Sir Hamish? Victor Perez at your service.'

Sir Hamish was dumbfounded. He simply stood and stared at the middle-aged little Mexican who had arrived for dinner dressed in a grubby white T-shirt and Western jeans. Perez looked as if he hadn't shaved for three days and reminded Sir Hamish of those bandits he had seen in B-movies when he was a schoolboy. He wore a heavy gold bracelet around his wrist that could have come from Cartier's and a tiger's tooth on a platinum chain around his neck that looked as if it had come from Woolworth's. Perez grinned from ear to ear, pleased with the effect he was making.

'Good evening,' replied Sir Hamish stiffly, taking a step backwards. 'Would you care for a sherry?'

'No, thank you, Sir Hamish. I've grown into the habit of liking your whisky, on the rocks with a little soda.'

'I'm sorry, I only have . . . '

'Don't worry, sir, I have some in my room,' said David Heath, and rushed away to retrieve a bottle of Johnnie Walker he had hidden under the shirts in his top drawer. Despite this Scottish aid, the conversation before dinner among the three men was somewhat stilted, but David Heath had not come five thousand miles for an inferior hotel meal with Victor Perez, and Victor Perez in any other circumstances would not have crossed the road to meet Sir Hamish Graham, even if he'd built it. Their conversation ranged from the recent visit to Mexico of Her Majesty The Queen — as Sir Hamish referred to her — to the proposed return trip of President Portillo to Britain. Dinner might have gone more smoothly if Mr Perez hadn't eaten most of the food with his hands and then proceeded to wipe his fingers on his jeans. The more Sir Hamish stared at him in disbelief, the more the little

Mexican would grin from ear to ear. After dinner David Heath thought the time had come to steer the conversation towards the real purpose of the meeting, but not before Sir Hamish had reluctantly had to call for a bottle of brandy and a box of cigars.

'We are looking for an agent to represent the Graham Construction Company in Mexico, Mr Perez, and you have been highly recommended,' said Sir Hamish, sounding unconvinced by his own statement.

'Do call me Victor.'

Sir Hamish bowed silently and shuddered. There was no way this man was going to be allowed to call him Hamish.

'I'd be pleased to represent you, Hamish,' continued Perez, 'provided that you find my terms acceptable.'

'Perhaps you could enlighten us as to what those — hm, terms — might be,' said Sir Hamish stiffly.

'Certainly,' said the little Mexican cheerfully. 'I require ten per cent of the agreed tender figure, five per cent to be paid on the day you are awarded the contract and five per cent whenever you present your completion certificates. Not a penny to be paid until you have received your fee, all my payments deposited in an account at Credit Suisse in Geneva within seven days of the National Bank of Mexico clearing your cheque.'

David Heath drew in his breath sharply and stared down at the stone floor.

'But under those terms you would make nearly four million dollars,' protested Sir

Hamish, now red in the face. 'That's over half our projected profit.'

'That, as I believe you say in England, Hamish, is your problem. You fixed the tender price,' said Perez, 'not me. In any case, there's still enough in the deal for both of us to make a handsome profit, which is surely fair, as we bring half the equation to the table.'

Sir Hamish was speechless as he fiddled with his bow tie. David Heath examined his fingernails attentively.

'Think the whole thing over, Hamish,' said Victor Perez, sounding unperturbed, 'and let me know your decision by midday tomorrow. The outcome makes little difference to me.' The Mexican rose, shook hands with Sir Hamish and left. David Heath, sweating slightly, accompanied him down in the lift. In the foyer he clasped hands damply with the Mexican.

'Good night, Victor. I'm sure everything will be all right — by midday tomorrow.'

'I hope so,' replied the Mexican, 'for your sake.' He strolled out of the foyer whistling.

Sir Hamish, a glass of water in his hand, was still seated at the dinner table when his project manager returned.

'I do not believe it is possible that that — that that man can represent the Secretary of State, represent a government minister.'

'I am assured that he does,' replied David Heath.

'But to part with nearly four million dollars to such an individual . . .'

'I agree with you, sir, but that is the way

business is conducted out here.'

'I can't believe it,' said Sir Hamish. 'I *won't* believe it. I want you to make an appointment for me to see the minister first thing tomorrow morning.'

'He won't like that, sir. It might expose his position, and put him right out in the open in a way that could only embarrass him.'

'I don't give a damn about embarrassing him. We are discussing a bribe, do I have to spell it out for you, Heath? A bribe of nearly four million dollars. Have you no principles, man?'

'Yes, sir, but I would still advise you against seeing the Secretary of State. He won't want any of your conversation with Mr Perez on the record.'

'I have run this company my way for nearly thirty years, Mr Heath, and I shall be the judge of what I want on the record.'

'Yes, of course, sir.'

'I will see the Secretary of State first thing in the morning. Kindly arrange a meeting.'

'If you insist, sir,' said David Heath resignedly.

'I insist.'

The project manager departed to his own room and a sleepless night. Early the next morning he delivered a handwritten, personal and private letter to the minister, who sent a car round immediately for the Scottish industrialist.

Sir Hamish was driven slowly through the noisy, exuberant, bustling crowds of the city in the minister's black Ford Galaxy with flag flying. People made way for the car respectfully. The chauffeur came to a halt outside the Ministry of

Buildings and Public Works in Paseo de la Reforma and guided Sir Hamish through the long white corridors to a waiting room. A few minutes later an assistant showed Sir Hamish through to the Secretary of State and took a seat by his side. The minister, a severe-looking man who appeared to be well into his seventies, was dressed in an immaculate white suit, white shirt and blue tie. He rose, leaned over the vast expanse of green leather and offered his hand.

'Do have a seat, Sir Hamish.'

'Thank you,' the chairman said, feeling more at home as he took in the minister's office; on the ceiling a large propeller-like fan revolved slowly, making little difference to the stuffiness of the room, while hanging on the wall behind the minister was a signed picture of President José Lopez Portillo in full morning dress, and below the photo a plaque displayed a coat of arms.

'I see you were educated at Cambridge.'

'That is correct, Sir Hamish, I was at Corpus Christi for three years.'

'Then you know my country well, sir.'

'I do have many happy memories of my stays in England, Sir Hamish; in fact, I still visit London as often as my leave allows.'

'You must take a trip to Edinburgh some time.'

'I have already done so, Sir Hamish. I attended the Festival on two occasions and now know why your city is described as the Athens of the north.'

'You are well informed, Minister.'

'Thank you, Sir Hamish. Now I must ask how I can help you. Your assistant's note was rather vague.'

'First let me say, Minister, that my company is honoured to be considered for the city ring-road project, and I hope that our experience of thirty years in construction, twenty of them in the Third World' — he nearly said the undeveloped countries, an expression his project manager had warned him against — 'is the reason you, as minister in charge, found us the natural choice for this contract.'

'That, and your reputation for finishing a job on time at the stipulated price,' replied the Secretary of State. 'Only twice in your history have you returned to the principal asking for changes in the payment schedule. Once in Uganda when you were held up by Amin's pathetic demands, and the other project, if I remember rightly, was in Bolivia, an airport, when you were unavoidably delayed for six months because of an earthquake. In both cases, you completed the contract at the new price stipulated, and my advisers think you must have lost money on both occasions.' The Secretary of State mopped his brow with a silk handkerchief before continuing. 'I would not wish you to think my government takes these decisions of selection lightly.'

Sir Hamish was astounded by the Secretary of State's command of his brief, the more so as no prompting notes lay on the leather-topped desk in front of him. He suddenly felt guilty at the little he knew about the Secretary of State's background or history.

'Of course not, Minister. I am flattered by your personal concern, which makes me all the more determined to broach an embarrassing subject that has . . . '

'Before you say anything else, Sir Hamish, may I ask you some questions?'

'Of course, Minister.'

'Do you still find the tender price of $39,121,110 acceptable in *all* the circumstances?'

'Yes, Minister.'

'That amount still leaves you enough to do a worthwhile job while making a profit for your company?'

'Yes, Minister, but . . . '

'Excellent, then I think all you have to decide is whether you want to sign the contract by midday today.' The minister emphasised the word 'midday' as clearly as he could.

Sir Hamish, who had never understood the expression 'a nod is as good as a wink,' charged foolishly on.

'There is, nevertheless, one aspect of the contract I feel that I should discuss with you privately.'

'Are you sure that would be wise, Sir Hamish?'

Sir Hamish hesitated, but only for a moment, before proceeding. Had David Heath heard the conversation that had taken place so far, he would have stood up, shaken hands with the Secretary of State, removed the top of his fountain pen and headed towards the contract — but not his employer.

'Yes, Minister, I feel I must,' said Sir Hamish firmly.

'Will you kindly leave us, Miss Vieites?' said the Secretary of State.

The assistant closed her shorthand book, rose and left the room. Sir Hamish waited for the door to close before he began again.

'Yesterday I had a visit from a countryman of yours, a Mr Victor Perez, who resides here in Mexico City and claims — '

'An excellent man,' said the minister very quietly.

Still Sir Hamish charged on. 'Yes, I daresay he is, Minister, but he asked to be allowed to represent Graham Construction as our agent, and I wondered — '

'A common practice in Mexico, no more than is required by the law,' said the minister, swinging his chair round and staring out of the window.

'Yes, I appreciate that is the custom,' said Sir Hamish, now talking to the minister's back, 'but if I am to part with ten per cent of the government's money I must be convinced that such a decision meets with your personal approval.' Sir Hamish thought he had worded that rather well.

'Um,' said the Secretary of State, measuring his words, 'Victor Perez is a good man and has always been loyal to the Mexican cause. Perhaps he leaves an unfortunate impression sometimes, not out of what you would call the 'top drawer', Sir Hamish, but then we have no class barriers in Mexico.' The minister swung back to face Sir Hamish.

The Scottish industrialist flushed. 'Of course

not, Minister, but that, if you will forgive me, is hardly the point. Mr Perez is asking me to hand over nearly four million dollars, which is over half of my estimated profit on the project without allowing for any contingencies or mishaps that might occur later.'

'You chose the tender figure, Sir Hamish. I confess I was amused by the fact you added your date of birth to the thirty-nine million.'

Sir Hamish's mouth opened wide.

'I would have thought,' continued the minister, 'given your record over the past three years and the present situation in Britain, you were not in a position to be fussy.'

The minister gazed impassively at Sir Hamish's startled face. Both started to speak at the same time. Sir Hamish swallowed his words.

'Allow me to tell you a little story about Victor Perez. When the war was at its fiercest' (the old Secretary of State was referring to the Mexican Revolution, in the same way that an American thinks of Vietnam or a Briton of Germany when they hear the word 'war'), 'Victor's father was one of the young men under my command who died on the battlefield at Celaya only a few days before victory was ours. He left a son born on the day of independence who never knew his father. I have the honour, Sir Hamish, to be godfather to that child. We christened him Victor.'

'I can understand that you have a responsibility to an old comrade, but I still feel four million is — '

'Do you? Then let me continue. Just before Victor's father died I visited him in a field hospital, and he asked only that I should take care of his wife. She died in childbirth. I therefore considered my responsibility passed on to their only child.'

Sir Hamish remained silent for a moment. 'I appreciate your attitude, Minister, but ten per cent of one of your largest contracts?'

'One day,' continued the Secretary of State, as if he had not heard Sir Hamish's comment, 'Victor's father was fighting in the front line at Zacatecas, and looking out across a minefield he saw a young lieutenant lying face down in the mud with his leg nearly blown off. With no thought for his own safety, he crawled through that minefield until he reached the lieutenant, and then he dragged him yard by yard back to the camp. It took him over three hours. He then carried the lieutenant to a truck and drove him to the nearest field hospital, undoubtedly saving his leg, and probably his life. So you see, the government have good cause to allow Perez's son the privilege of representing them from time to time.'

'I agree with you, Minister,' said Sir Hamish quietly. 'Quite admirable.'

The Secretary of State smiled for the first time.

'But I still confess I cannot understand why you allow him such a large percentage.'

The minister frowned. 'I am afraid, Sir Hamish, if you cannot understand that, you can never hope to understand the principles we Mexicans live by.'

The Secretary of State rose from behind his desk, limped to the door and showed Sir Hamish out.

The Perfect Gentleman

I would never have met Edward Shrimpton if he hadn't needed a towel. He stood naked by my side staring down at a bench in front of him, muttering, 'I could have sworn I left the damn thing there.'

I had just come out of the sauna, swathed in towels, so I took one off my shoulder and passed it to him. He thanked me and put out his hand.

'Edward Shrimpton,' he said smiling. I took his hand and wondered what we must have looked like standing there in the gymnasium locker room of the Metropolitan Club in the early evening, two grown men shaking hands in the nude.

'I don't remember seeing you in the club before,' he added.

'No, I'm an overseas member.'

'Ah, from England. What brings you to New York?'

'I'm pursuing an American novelist whom my company would like to publish in England.'

'And are you having any success?'

'Yes, I think I'll close the deal this week — as long as the agent stops trying to convince me that his author is a cross between Tolstoy and Dickens and should be paid accordingly.'

'Neither was paid particularly well, if I remember correctly,' offered Edward Shrimpton as he energetically rubbed the towel up and down his back.

'A fact I pointed out to the agent at the time, who countered by reminding me that it was my House which published Dickens originally.'

'I suggest,' said Edward Shrimpton, 'that you remind him that the end result turned out to be successful for all concerned.'

'I did, but I fear this agent is more interested in 'up front' than posterity.'

'As a banker that's a sentiment of which I could hardly disapprove, as the one thing we have in common with publishers is that our clients are always trying to tell us a good tale.'

'Perhaps you should sit down and write one of them for me?' I said politely.

'Heaven forbid, you must be sick of being told that there's a book in every one of us so I hasten to assure you that there isn't one in me.'

I laughed, as I found it refreshing not to be informed by a new acquaintance that his memoirs, if only he could find the time to write them, would overnight be one of the world's bestsellers.

'Perhaps there's a story in you, but you're just not aware of it,' I suggested.

'If that's the case, I'm afraid it's passed me by.'

Mr Shrimpton re-emerged from behind the row of little tin cubicles and handed me back my towel. He was now fully dressed and stood, I would have guessed, a shade under six feet. He wore a Wall Street banker's pinstripe suit and, although he was nearly bald, he had a remarkable physique for a man who must have been well into his sixties. Only his thick white moustache gave away his true age, and would have been more in keeping with a retired English colonel than a New York banker.

'Are you going to be in New York long?' he inquired, as he took a small leather case from his inside pocket and removed a pair of half-moon spectacles and placed them on the end of his nose.

'Just for the week.'

'I don't suppose you're free for lunch tomorrow, by any chance?' he inquired, peering over the top of his glasses.

'Yes, I am. I certainly can't face another meal with that agent.'

'Good, good, then why don't you join me and I can follow the continuing drama of capturing the elusive American Author?'

'And perhaps I'll discover there is a story in you after all.'

'Not a hope,' he said, 'you would be backing a loser if you depend on that,' and once again he offered his hand. 'One o'clock, members' dining room suit you?'

'One o'clock, members' dining room,' I repeated.

As he left the locker room I walked over to the mirror and straightened my tie. I was dining that night with Eric McKenzie, a publishing friend, who had originally proposed me for membership of the club. To be accurate, Eric McKenzie was a friend of my father rather than myself. They had met just before the war while on holiday in Portugal and when I was elected to the club, soon after my father's retirement, Eric took it upon himself to have dinner with me whenever I was in New York. One's parents' generation never see one as anything but a child who will always be in need of constant care and attention. As he was a contemporary of my father, Eric must have been nearly seventy and, although hard of hearing and slightly bent, he was always amusing and good company, even if he did continually ask me if I was aware that his grandfather was Scottish.

As I strapped on my watch, I checked that he was due to arrive in a few minutes. I put on my jacket and strolled out into the hall to find that he was already there, waiting for me. Eric was killing time by reading the out-of-date club notices. Americans, I have observed, can always be relied upon to arrive early or late; never on time. I stood staring at the stooping man, whose hair but for a few strands had now turned silver. His three-piece suit had a button missing on the jacket which reminded me that his wife had died last year. After another thrust-out hand and exchange of welcomes, we took the lift to the second floor and walked to the dining room.

The members' dining room at the Metropolitan differs little from any other men's club. It has a fair sprinkling of old leather chairs, old carpets, old portraits and old members. A waiter guided us to a corner table which overlooked Central Park. We ordered, and then settled back to discuss all the subjects I found I usually cover with an acquaintance I only have the chance to catch up with a couple of times a year — our families, children, mutual friends, work; baseball and cricket. By the time we had reached cricket we had also reached coffee, so we strolled down to the far end of the room and made ourselves comfortable in two well-worn leather chairs. When the coffee arrived I ordered two brandies and watched Eric unwrap a large Cuban cigar. Although they displayed a West Indian band on the outside, I knew they were Cuban because I had picked them up for him from a tobacconist in St James's, Piccadilly, which specialises in changing the labels for its American customers. I have often thought that they must be the only shop in the world that changes labels with the sole purpose of making a superior product appear inferior. I am certain my wine merchant does it the other way round.

While Eric was attempting to light the cigar, my eyes wandered to a board on the wall. To be more accurate it was a highly polished wooden plaque with oblique golden lettering painted on it, honouring those men who over the years had won the club's backgammon championship. I glanced idly down the list, not expecting to see anybody with whom I would be familiar, when I was brought up by the name of Edward Shrimpton. Once in the late thirties he had been the runner-up.

'That's interesting,' I said.

'What is?' asked Eric, now wreathed in enough smoke to have puffed himself out of Grand Central Station.

'Edward Shrimpton was runner-up in the club's backgammon championship in the late thirties. I'm having lunch with him tomorrow.'

'I didn't realise you knew him.'

'I didn't until this afternoon,' I said, and then explained how we had met.

Eric laughed and turned to stare up at the board. Then he added, rather mysteriously: 'That's a night I'm never like to forget.'

'Why?' I asked.

Eric hesitated, and looked uncertain of himself before continuing: 'Too much water has passed under the bridge for anyone to care now.' He paused again, as a hot piece of ash fell to the floor and added to the burn marks that made their own private pattern in the carpet. 'Just before the war Edward Shrimpton was among the best half-dozen backgammon players in the world. In fact, it must have been around that time he won the unofficial world championship in Monte Carlo.'

'And he couldn't win the club championship?'

' 'Couldn't' would be the wrong word, dear boy. 'Didn't' might be more accurate.' Eric lapsed into another preoccupied silence.

'Are you going to explain?' I asked, hoping he would continue, 'or am I to be left like a child who wants to know who killed Cock Robin?'

'All in good time, but first allow me to get this damn cigar started.'

I remained silent, and four matches later, he said, 'Before I begin, take a look at the man sitting over there in the corner with the young blonde.'

I turned and glanced back towards the dining room area, and saw a man attacking a porterhouse steak. He looked about the same age as Eric and wore a smart new suit that was unable to disguise that he had a weight problem: only his tailor could have smiled at him with any pleasure. He was seated opposite a slight, not unattractive strawberry blonde of half his age who could have trodden on a beetle and failed to crush it.

'What an unlikely pair. Who are they?'

'Harry Newman and his fourth wife. They're always the same. The wives I mean — blonde hair, blue eyes, ninety pounds, and dumb. I can never understand why any man gets divorced only to marry a carbon copy of the original.'

'Where does Edward Shrimpton fit into the jigsaw?' I asked, trying to guide Eric back on to the subject.

'Patience, patience,' said my host, as he relit his cigar for the second time. 'At your age you've far more time to waste than I have.'

I laughed and picked up the cognac nearest to me and swirled the brandy around in my cupped hands.

'Harry Newman,' continued Eric, now almost hidden in smoke, 'was the fellow who beat Edward Shrimpton in the final of the club championship that year, although in truth he was never in the same class as Edward.'

'Do explain,' I said, as I looked up at the board to check that it was Newman's name that preceded Edward Shrimpton's.

'Well,' said Eric, 'after the semi-final, which Edward had won with consummate ease, we all assumed the final would only be a formality.

Harry had always been a good player, but as I had been the one to lose to him in the semi-finals, I knew he couldn't hope to survive a contest with Edward Shrimpton. The club final is won by the first man to twenty-one points, and if I had been asked for an opinion at the time I would have reckoned the result would end up around 21–5 in Edward's favour. Damn cigar,' he said, and lit it for a fourth time. Once again I waited impatiently.

'The final is always held on a Saturday night, and poor Harry over there,' said Eric, pointing his cigar towards the far corner of the room while depositing some more ash on the floor, 'who all of us thought was doing rather well in the insurance business, had a bankruptcy notice served on him the Monday morning before the final — I might add through no fault of his own. His partner had cashed in his stock without Harry's knowledge, disappeared, and left him with all the bills to pick up. Everyone in the club was sympathetic.

'On the Thursday the press got hold of the story, and for good measure they added that Harry's wife had run off with the partner. Harry didn't show his head in the club all week, and some of us wondered if he would scratch from the final and let Edward win by default as the result was such a foregone conclusion anyway. But the Games Committee received no communication from Harry to suggest the contest was off so they proceeded as though nothing had happened. On the night of the final, I dined with Edward Shrimpton here in the club. He was in fine form. He ate very little and drank nothing but a glass of water. If you had asked me then I wouldn't have put a penny on Harry Newman even if the odds had been ten to one.

'We all dined upstairs on the third floor, as the Committee had cleared this room so that they could seat sixty in a square around the board. The final was due to start at nine o'clock. By twenty to nine there wasn't a seat left in the place, and members were already standing two deep behind the square: it wasn't every day we had the chance to see a world champion in action. By five to nine, Harry still hadn't turned up and some of the members were beginning to get a little restless. As nine o'clock chimed, the referee went over to Edward and had a word with him. I saw Edward shake his head in disagreement and walk away. Just at the point, when I thought the referee would have to be firm and award the match to Edward, Harry strolled in looking very dapper adorned in a dinner jacket several sizes smaller than the suit he is wearing tonight. Edward went straight up to him, shook him warmly by the hand and together they walked into the centre of the room. Even with the throw of the first dice there was a tension about that match. Members were waiting to see how Harry would fare in the opening game.'

The intermittent cigar went out again. I leaned over and struck a match for him.

'Thank you, dear boy. Now, where was I? Oh, yes, the first game. Well, Edward only just won the first game and I wondered if he wasn't concentrating or if perhaps he had become a little too relaxed while waiting for his opponent. In the second game the dice ran well for Harry and he won fairly easily. From that moment on it became a finely fought battle, and by the time the score had reached 11–9 in Edward's favour the tension in the room was quite electric. By the ninth game I began watching more carefully and noticed that Edward allowed himself to be drawn into a back game, a small error in judgement that only a seasoned player would have spotted. I wondered how many more subtle errors had already passed that I hadn't observed. Harry went on to win the ninth, making the score 18-17 in his favour. I watched even more diligently as Edward did just enough to win the tenth game and, with a rash double, just enough to lose the eleventh, bring the score to 20 all, so that everything would depend on the final game. I swear that nobody had left the room that evening, and not one back remained against a chair; some members were even hanging on to the window ledges. The room was now full of drink and thick with cigar smoke, and yet when Harry picked up the dice cup for the last game you could hear the little squares of ivory rattle before they hit the board. The dice ran well for Harry in that final game and Edward only made one small error early on that I was able to pick up; but it was enough to give Harry game, match and championship. After the last throw of the dice everyone in that room, including Edward, gave the new champion a standing ovation.'

'Had many other members worked out what

had really happened that night?'

'No, I don't think so,' said Eric. 'And certainly Harry Newman hadn't. The talk afterwards was that Harry had never played a better game in his life, and what a worthy champion he was, all the more for the difficulties he laboured under.'

'Did Edward have anything to say?'

'Toughest match he'd been in since Monte Carlo, and only hoped he would be given the chance to avenge the defeat next year.'

'But he wasn't,' I said, looking up again at the board. 'He never won the club championship.'

'That's right. After Roosevelt had insisted we help you guys out in England, the club didn't hold the competition again until 1946, and by then Edward had been to war and had lost all interest in the game.'

'And Harry?'

'Oh, Harry. Harry never looked back after that; must have made a dozen deals in the club that night. Within a year he was on top again, even found himself another cute little blonde.'

'What does Edward say about the result now, thirty years later?'

'Do you know, that remains a mystery to this day. I have never heard him mention the game once in all that time.'

Eric's cigar had come to the end of its working life and he stubbed the remains out in an ashless ashtray. It obviously acted as a signal to remind him that it was time to go home. He rose a little unsteadily and I walked down with him to the front door.

'Goodbye, my boy,' he said, 'do give Edward

my best wishes when you have lunch with him tomorrow. And remember not to play him at backgammon. He'd still kill you.'

* * *

The next day I arrived in the front hall a few minutes before our appointed time, not sure if Edward Shrimpton would fall into the category of early or late Americans. As she clock struck one, he walked through the door: there has to be an exception to every rule. We agreed to go straight up to lunch since he had to be back in Wall Street for a two-thirty appointment. We stepped into the packed lift, and I pressed the No. 3 button. The doors closed like a tired concertina and the slowest lift in America made its way towards the second floor.

As we entered the dining room, I was amused to see Harry Newman was already there, attacking another steak, while the little blonde lady was nibbling a salad. He waved expansively at Edward Shrimpton, who returned the gesture with a friendly nod. We sat down at a table in the centre of the room and studied the menu. Steak and kidney pie was the dish of the day, which was probably the case in half the men's clubs in the world. Edward wrote down our orders in a neat and legible hand on the little white slip provided by the waiter.

Edward asked me about the author I was chasing and made some penetrating comments about her earlier work, to which I responded as best I could while trying to think of a plot to make him discuss the pre-war backgammon championship, which I considered would make a far better story than anything she had ever written. But he never talked about himself once during the meal, so I despaired. Finally, staring up at the plaque on the wall, I said clumsily:

'I see you were runner-up in the club backgammon championship just before the war. You must have been a fine player.'

'No, not really,' he replied. 'Not many people bothered about the game in those days. There is a different attitude today with all the youngsters taking it so seriously.'

'What about the champion?' I said, pushing my luck.

'Harry Newman? He was an outstanding player, and particularly good under pressure. He's the gentleman who greeted us when we came in. That's him sitting over there in the corner with his wife.'

I looked obediently towards Mr Newman's table but my host added nothing more so I gave up. We ordered coffee and that would have been the end of Edward's story if Harry Newman and his wife had not headed straight for us after they had finished their lunch. Edward was on his feet long before I was, despite my twenty-year advantage. Harry Newman looked even bigger standing up, and his little blonde wife looked more like the dessert than his spouse.

'Ed,' he boomed, 'how are you?'

'I'm well, thank you, Harry,' Edward replied. 'May I introduce my guest?'

'Nice to know you,' he said. 'Rusty, I've always

wanted you to meet Ed Shrimpton, because I've talked to you about him so often in the past.'

'Have you, Harry?' she squeaked.

'Of course. You remember, honey. Ed is up there on the backgammon honours board,' he said, pointing a stubby finger towards the plaque. 'With only one name in front of him, and that's mine. And Ed was the world champion at the time. Isn't that right, Ed?'

'That's right, Harry.'

'So I suppose I really should have been the world champion that year, wouldn't you say?'

'I couldn't quarrel with that conclusion,' replied Edward.

'On the big day, Rusty, when it really mattered, and the pressure was on, I beat him fair and square.'

I stood in silent disbelief as Edward Shrimpton still volunteered no disagreement.

'We must play again for old times' sake, Ed,' the fat man continued. 'It would be fun to see if you could beat me now. Mind you, I'm a bit rusty nowadays, Rusty.' He laughed loudly at his own joke, but his spouse's face remained blank. I wondered how long it would be before there was a fifth Mrs Newman.

'It's been great to see you again, Ed. Take care of yourself.'

'Thank you Harry,' said Edward.

We both sat down again as Newman and his wife left the dining room. Our coffee was now cold so we ordered a fresh pot. The room was almost empty and when I had poured two cups for us Edward leaned over to me conspiratorially and whispered: 'Now there's a hell of a story for a publisher like you,' he said. 'I mean the real truth about Harry Newman.'

My ears pricked up as I anticipated his version of the story of what had actually happened on the night of that pre-war backgammon championship over thirty years before.

'Really?' I said, innocently.

'Oh, yes,' said Edward. 'It was not as simple as you might think. Just before the war Harry was let down very badly by his business partner, who not only stole his money, but for good measure his wife as well. The very week that he was at his lowest he won the club backgammon championship, put all his troubles behind him and, against the odds, made a brilliant comeback. You know, he's worth a fortune today. Now, wouldn't you agree that that would make one hell of a story?'

À La Carte

Arthur Hapgood was demobbed on November 3rd, 1946. Within a month he was back at his old workplace on the shop-floor of the Triumph factory on the outskirts of Coventry.

The five years spent in the Sherwood Foresters, four of them as a quartermaster seconded to a tank regiment, only underlined Arthur's likely post-war fate, despite having hoped to find more rewarding work once the war was over. However, on returning to England he quickly discovered that in a 'land fit for heroes' jobs were not that easy to come by, and although he did not want to go back to the work he had done for five years before war had been declared, that of fitting wheels on cars, he reluctantly, after four weeks on the dole, went to see his former works' manager at Triumph.

'The job's yours if you want it, Arthur,' the works' manager assured him.

'And the future?'

'The car's no longer a toy for the eccentric rich or even just a necessity for the businessman,' the works' manager replied. 'In fact,' he continued, 'management are preparing for the 'two-car family'.'

'So they'll need even more wheels to be put on cars,' said Arthur forlornly.

'That's the ticket.'

Arthur signed on within the hour and it was

only a matter of days before he was back into his old routine. After all, he often reminded his wife, it didn't take a degree in engineering to screw four knobs on to a wheel a hundred times a shift.

Arthur soon accepted the fact that he would have to settle for second best. However, second best was not what he planned for his son.

Mark had celebrated his fifth birthday before his father had even set eyes on him, but from the moment Arthur returned home he lavished everything he could on the boy.

* * *

Arthur was determined that Mark was not going to end up working on the shop-floor of a car factory for the rest of his life. He put in hours of overtime to earn enough money to ensure that the boy could have extra tuition in maths, general science and English. He felt well rewarded when the boy passed his eleven-plus and won a place at King Henry VIII Grammar School, and that pride did not falter when Mark went on to pass five O levels and two years later added two A levels.

Arthur tried not to show his disappointment when, on Mark's eighteenth birthday, the boy informed him that he did not want to go to university.

'What kind of career are you hoping to take up then, lad?' Arthur enquired.

'I've filled in an application form to join you on the shop-floor just as soon as I leave school.'

'But why would you — '

'Why not? Most of my friends who're leaving this term have already been accepted by Triumph, and they can't wait to get started.'

'You must be out of your mind.'

'Come off it, Dad. The pay's good and you've shown that there's always plenty of extra money to be picked up with overtime. And I don't mind hard work.'

'Do you think I spent all those years making sure you got a first-class education just to let you end up like me, putting wheels on cars for the rest of your life?' Arthur shouted.

'That's not the whole job and you know it, Dad.'

'You go there over my dead body,' said his father. 'I don't care what your friends end up doing, I only care about you. You could be a solicitor, an accountant, an army officer, even a schoolmaster. Why should you want to end up at a car factory?'

'It's better paid than schoolmastering for a start,' said Mark. 'My French master once told me that he wasn't as well off as you.'

'That's not the point, lad — '

'The point is, Dad, I can't be expected to spend the rest of my life doing a job I don't enjoy just to satisfy one of your fantasies.'

'Well, I'm not going to allow you to waste the rest of your life,' said Arthur, getting up from the breakfast table. 'The first thing I'm going to do when I get in to work this morning is see that your application is turned down.'

'That isn't fair, Dad. I have the right to — '

But his father had already left the room, and

did not utter another word to the boy before leaving for the factory.

For over a week father and son didn't speak to each other. It was Mark's mother who was left to come up with the compromise. Mark could apply for any job that met with his father's approval and as long as he completed a year at that job he could, if he still wanted to, reapply to work at the factory. His father for his part would not then put any obstacle in his son's way.

Arthur nodded. Mark also reluctantly agreed to the solution.

'But only if you complete the full year,' Arthur warned solemnly.

During those last days of the summer holiday Arthur came up with several suggestions for Mark to consider, but the boy showed no enthusiasm for any of them. Mark's mother became quite anxious that her son would end up with no job at all until while helping her slice potatoes for dinner one night, Mark confided that he thought hotel management seemed the least unattractive proposition he had considered so far.

'At least you'd have a roof over your head and be regularly fed,' his mother said.

'Bet they don't cook as well as you, Mum,' said Mark as he placed the sliced potatoes on the top of the Lancashire hot-pot. 'Still, it's only a year.'

During the next month Mark attended several interviews at hotels around the country without success. It was then that his father discovered that his old company sergeant was head porter at the Savoy: immediately Arthur started to pull a few strings.

'If the boy's any good,' Arthur's old comrade-in-arms assured him over a pint, 'he could end up as a head porter, even a hotel manager.' Arthur seemed well satisfied, even though Mark was still assuring his friends that he would be joining them a year to the day.

On September 1st, 1959, Arthur and Mark Hapgood travelled together by bus to Coventry station. Arthur shook hands with the boy and promised him, 'Your mother and I will make sure it's a special Christmas this year when they give you your first leave. And don't worry — you'll be in good hands with 'Sarge'. He'll teach you a thing or two. Just remember to keep your nose clean.'

Mark said nothing and returned a thin smile as he boarded the train. 'You'll never regret it . . .' were the last words Mark heard his father say as the train pulled out of the station.

* * *

Mark regretted it from the moment he set foot in the hotel.

As a junior porter he started his day at six in the morning and ended at six in the evening. He was entitled to a fifteen-minute mid-morning break, a forty-five-minute lunch break and another fifteen-minute break around mid-afternoon. After the first month had passed he could not recall when he had been granted all three breaks on the same day, and he quickly learned that there was no one to whom he could protest. His duties consisted of carrying guests' cases up to their rooms, then lugging them back down again the moment they wanted to leave. With an average of three hundred people staying in the hotel each night the process was endless. The pay turned out to be half what his friends were getting back home and as he had to hand over all his tips to the head porter, however much overtime Mark put in, he never saw an extra penny. On the only occasion he dared to mention it to the head porter he was met with the words, 'Your time will come, lad.'

It did not worry Mark that his uniform didn't fit or that his room was six foot by six foot and overlooked Charing Cross Station, or even that he didn't get a share of the tips; but it did worry him that there was nothing he could do to please the head porter — however clean he kept his nose.

Sergeant Crann, who considered the Savoy nothing more than an extension of his old platoon, didn't have a lot of time for young men under his command who hadn't done their national service.

'But I wasn't *eligible* to do national service,' insisted Mark. 'No one born after 1939 was called up.'

'Don't make excuses, lad.'

'It's not an excuse, Sarge. It's the truth.'

'And don't call me 'Sarge'. I'm 'Sergeant Crann' to you, and don't you forget it.'

'Yes, Sergeant Crann.'

At the end of each day Mark would return to

his little box-room with its small bed, small chair and tiny chest of drawers, and collapse exhausted. The only picture in the room — of the Laughing Cavalier — was on the calendar that hung above Mark's bed. The date of September 1st, 1960, was circled in red to remind him when he would be allowed to rejoin his friends at the factory back home. Each night before falling asleep he would cross out the offending day like a prisoner making scratch marks on a wall.

At Christmas Mark returned home for a four-day break, and when his mother saw the general state of the boy she tried to talk his father into allowing Mark to give up the job early, but Arthur remained implacable.

'We made an agreement. I can't be expected to get him a job at the factory if he isn't responsible enough to keep to his part of a bargain.'

During the holiday Mark waited for his friends outside the factory gate until their shift had ended and listened to their stories of weekends spent watching football, drinking at the pub and dancing to the Everly Brothers. They all sympathised with his problem and looked forward to him joining them in September. 'It's only a few more months,' one of them reminded him cheerfully.

Far too quickly, Mark was on the journey back to London, where he continued unwillingly to hump cases up and down the hotel corridors for month after month.

Once the English rain had subsided the usual

influx of American tourists began. Mark liked the Americans, who treated him as an equal and often tipped him a shilling when others would have given him only sixpence. But whatever the amount Mark received Sergeant Crann would still pocket it with the inevitable, 'Your time will come, lad.'

One such American for whom Mark ran around diligently every day during his fortnight's stay ended up presenting the boy with a ten-bob note as he left the front entrance of the hotel.

Mark said, 'Thank you, sir,' and turned round to see Sergeant Crann standing in his path.

'Hand it over,' said Crann as soon as the American visitor was well out of earshot.

'I was going to the moment I saw you,' said Mark, passing the note to his superior.

'Not thinking of pocketing what's rightfully mine, was you?'

'No, I wasn't,' said Mark. 'Though God knows I earned it.'

'Your time will come, lad,' said Sergeant Crann without much thought.

'Not while someone as mean as you is in charge,' replied Mark sharply.

'What was that you said?' asked the head porter, veering round.

'You heard me the first time, Sarge.'

The clip across the ear took Mark by surprise.

'You, lad, have just lost your job. Nobody, but nobody, talks to me like that.' Sergeant Crann turned and set off smartly in the direction of the manager's office.

The hotel manager, Gerald Drummond,

listened to the head porter's version of events before asking Mark to report to his office immediately. 'You realise I have been left with no choice but to sack you,' were his first words once the door was closed.

Mark looked up at the tall, elegant man in his long, black coat, white collar and black tie. 'Am I allowed to tell you what actually happened, sir?' he asked.

Mr Drummond nodded, then listened without interruption as Mark gave his version of what had taken place that morning, and also disclosed the agreement he had entered into with his father. 'Please let me complete my final ten weeks,' Mark ended, 'or my father will only say I haven't kept my end of our bargain.'

'I haven't got another job vacant at the moment,' protested the manager. 'Unless you're willing to peel potatoes for ten weeks.'

'Anything,' said Mark.

'Then report to the kitchen at six tomorrow morning. I'll tell the third chef to expect you. Only if you think the head porter is a martinet just wait until you meet Jacques, our *maître chef de cuisine*. He won't clip your ear, he'll cut it off.'

Mark didn't care. He felt confident that for just ten weeks he could face anything, and at five-thirty the following morning he exchanged his dark blue uniform for a white top and blue and white check trousers before reporting for his new duties. To his surprise the kitchen took up almost the entire basement of the hotel, and was even more of a bustle than the lobby had been.

The third chef put him in the corner of the kitchen, next to a mountain of potatoes, a bowl of cold water and a sharp knife. Mark peeled through breakfast, lunch and dinner, and fell asleep on his bed that night without even enough energy left to cross a day off his calendar.

For the first week he never actually saw the fabled Jacques. With seventy people working in the kitchens Mark felt confident he could pass his whole period there without anyone being aware of him.

Each morning at six he would start peeling, then hand over the potatoes to a gangling youth called Terry who in turn would dice or cut them according to the third chef's instructions for the dish of the day. Monday sauté, Tuesday mashed, Wednesday French-fried, Thursday sliced, Friday roast, Saturday croquette . . . Mark quickly worked out a routine which kept him well ahead of Terry and therefore out of any trouble.

Having watched Terry do his job for over a week Mark felt sure he could have shown the young apprentice how to lighten his workload quite simply, but he decided to keep his mouth closed: opening it might only get him into more trouble, and he was certain the manager wouldn't give him a second chance.

Mark soon discovered that Terry always fell badly behind on Tuesday's shepherd's pie and Thursday's Lancashire hot-pot. From time to time the third chef would come across to complain and he would glance over at Mark to be sure that it wasn't him who was holding the process up. Mark made certain that he always had a spare tub of peeled potatoes by his side so that he escaped censure.

It was on the first Thursday morning in August (Lancashire hot-pot) that Terry sliced off the top of his forefinger. Blood spurted all over the sliced potatoes and on to the wooden table as the lad began yelling hysterically.

'Get him out of here!' Mark heard the *maître chef de cuisine* bellow above the noise of the kitchen as he stormed towards them.

'And you,' he said, pointing at Mark, 'clean up mess and start slicing rest of potatoes. I 'ave eight hundred hungry customers still expecting to feed.'

'Me?' said Mark in disbelief. 'But — '

'Yes, you. You couldn't do worse job than idiot who calls himself trainee chef and cuts off finger.' The chef marched away, leaving Mark to move reluctantly across to the table where Terry had been working. He felt disinclined to argue while the calendar was there to remind him that he was down to his last twenty-five days.

Mark set about a task he had carried out for his mother many times. The clean, neat cuts were delivered with a skill Terry would never learn to master. By the end of the day, although exhausted, Mark did not feel quite as tired as he had in the past.

At eleven that night the *maître chef de cuisine* threw off his hat and barged out of the swing doors, a sign to everyone else they could also leave the kitchen once everything that was their responsibility had been cleared up. A few seconds later the door swung back open and the chef burst in. He stared round the kitchen as everyone waited to see what he would do next. Having found what he was looking for, he headed straight for Mark.

'Oh, my God,' thought Mark. 'He's going to kill me.'

'How is your name?' the chef demanded.

'Mark Hapgood, sir,' he managed to splutter out.

'You waste on 'tatoes, Mark Hapgood,' said the chef. 'You start on vegetables in morning. Report at seven. If that *crétin* with half finger ever returns, put him to peeling 'tatoes.'

The chef turned on his heel even before Mark had the chance to reply. He dreaded the thought of having to spend three weeks in the middle of the kitchens, never once out of the *maître chef de cuisine*'s sight, but he accepted there was no alternative.

The next morning Mark arrived at six for fear of being late and spent an hour watching the fresh vegetables being unloaded from Covent Garden market. The hotel's supply manager checked every case carefully, rejecting several before he signed a chit to show the hotel had received over three thousand pounds' worth of vegetables. An average day, he assured Mark.

The *maître chef de cuisine* appeared a few minutes before seven-thirty, checked the menus and told Mark to score the Brussels sprouts, trim the French beans and remove the coarse outer leaves of the cabbages.

'But I don't know how,' Mark replied honestly. He could feel the other trainees in the kitchen edging away from him.

'Then I teach you,' roared the chef. 'Perhaps only thing you learn is if hope to be good chef, you able to do everyone's job in kitchen, even 'tato peeler's.'

'But I'm hoping to be a . . . ' Mark began and then thought better of it. The chef seemed not to have heard Mark as he took his place beside the new recruit. Everyone in the kitchen stared as the chef began to show Mark the basic skills of cutting, dicing and slicing.

'And remember other idiot's finger,' the chef said on completing the lesson and passing the razor-sharp knife back to Mark. 'Yours can be next.'

Mark started gingerly dicing the carrots, then the Brussels sprouts, removing the outer layer before cutting a firm cross in the stalk. Next he moved on to trimming and slicing the beans. Once again he found it fairly easy to keep ahead of the chef's requirements.

At the end of each day, after the head chef had left, Mark stayed on to sharpen all his knives in preparation for the following morning, and would not leave his work area until it was spotless.

On the sixth day, after a curt nod from the chef, Mark realised he must be doing something half-right. By the following Saturday he felt he had mastered the simple skills of vegetable preparation and found himself becoming fascinated by what the chef himself was up to. Although Jacques rarely addressed anyone as he marched round the acre of kitchen except to grunt his approval or disapproval — the latter more commonly — Mark quickly learned to anticipate his needs. Within a short space of time he began to feel that he was part of a team — even though he was only too aware of being the novice recruit.

On the deputy chef's day off the following week Mark was allowed to arrange the cooked vegetables in their bowls and spent some time making each dish look attractive as well as edible. The chef not only noticed but actually muttered his greatest accolade — '*Bon*.'

During his last three weeks at the Savoy Mark did not even look at the calendar above his bed.

One Thursday morning a message came down from the under-manager that Mark was to report to his office as soon as was convenient. Mark had quite forgotten that it was August 31st — his last day. He cut ten lemons into quarters, then finished preparing the forty plates of thinly sliced smoked salmon that would complete the first course for a wedding lunch. He looked with pride at his efforts before folding up his apron and leaving to collect his papers and final wage packet.

'Where you think you're going?' asked the chef, looking up.

'I'm off,' said Mark. 'Back to Conventry.'

'See you Monday then. You deserve day off.'

'No, I'm going home for good,' said Mark.

The chef stopped checking the cuts of rare beef that would make up the second course of the wedding feast.

‘Going?’ he repeated as if he didn’t understand the word.

‘Yes. I’ve finished my year and now I’m off home to work.’

‘I hope you found first-class hotel,’ said the chef with genuine interest.

‘I’m not going to work in a hotel.’

‘A restaurant, perhaps?’

‘No, I’m going to get a job at Triumph.’

The chef looked puzzled for a moment, unsure if it was his English or whether the boy was mocking him.

‘What is — Triumph?’

‘A place where they manufacture cars.’

‘You will manufacture cars?’

‘Not a whole car, but I will put the wheels on.’

‘You put cars on wheels?’ the chef said in disbelief.

‘No,’ laughed Mark. ‘Wheels on cars.’

The chef still looked uncertain.

‘So you will be cooking for the car workers?’

‘No. As I explained, I’m going to put the wheels on the cars,’ said Mark slowly, enunciating each word.

‘That not possible.’

‘Oh yes it is,’ responded Mark. ‘And I’ve waited a whole year to prove it.’

‘If I offered you job as commis chef, you change mind?’ asked the chef quietly.

‘Why would you do that?’

‘Because you ’ave talent in those fingers. In time I think you become chef, perhaps even good chef.’

‘No, thanks. I’m off to Coventry to join my mates.’

The head chef shrugged. '*Tant pis*,' he said, and without a second glance returned to the carcass of beef. He glanced over at the plates of smoked salmon. 'A wasted talent,' he added after the swing door had closed behind his potential protégé.

Mark locked his room, threw the calendar in the wastepaper basket and returned to the hotel to hand in his kitchen clothes to the housekeeper. The final action he took was to return his room key to the under-manager.

'Your wage packet, your cards and your PAYE. Oh, and the chef has phoned up to say he would be happy to give you a reference,' said the under-manager. 'Can't pretend that happens every day.'

'Won't need that where I'm going,' said Mark. 'But thanks all the same.'

He started off for the station at a brisk pace, his small battered suitcase swinging by his side, only to find that each step took a little longer. When he arrived at Euston he made his way to Platform 7 and began walking up and down, occasionally staring at the great clock above the booking hall. He watched first one train and then another pull out of the station bound for Coventry. He was aware of the station becoming dark as shadows filtered through the glass awning on to the public concourse. Suddenly he turned and walked off at an even brisker pace. If he hurried he could still be back in time to help chef prepare dinner that night.

* * *

Mark trained under Jacques le Rennue for five years. Vegetables were followed by sauces, fish by poultry, meats by pâtisserie. After eight years at the Savoy he was appointed second chef, and had learned so much from his mentor that regular patrons could no longer be sure when it was the *maître chef de cuisine*'s day off. Two years later Mark became a master chef, and when in 1971 Jacques was offered the opportunity to return to Paris and take over the kitchens of the George Cinq — an establishment that is to Paris what Harrods is to London — Jacques agreed, but only on condition that Mark accompanied him.

'It is wrong direction from Coventry,' Jacques warned him, 'and in any case they sure to offer you my job at the Savoy.'

'I'd better come along otherwise those Frogs will never get a decent meal.'

'Those Frogs,' said Jacques, 'will always know when it's my day off.'

'Yes, and book in even greater numbers,' suggested Mark, laughing.

It was not to be long before Parisians were flocking to the George Cinq, not to rest their weary heads but to relish the cooking of the two-chef team.

When Jacques celebrated his sixty-fifth birthday the great hotel did not have to look far to appoint his successor.

'The first Englishman ever to be *maître chef de cuisine* at the George Cinq,' said Jacques, raising a glass of champagne at his farewell banquet. 'Who would believe it? Of course, you will have to change your name to Marc to hold down such a position.'

'Neither will ever happen,' said Mark.

'Oh yes it will, because I 'ave recommended you.'

'Then I shall turn it down.'

'Going to put cars on wheels, *peut-être*?' asked Jacques mockingly.

'No, but I have found a little restaurant on the Left Bank. With my savings alone I can't quite afford the lease, but with your help . . . '

Chez Jacques opened on the rue du Plaisir on the Left Bank on May 1st, 1982, and it was not long before those customers who had taken the George Cinq for granted transferred their allegiance.

Mark's reputation spread as the two chefs pioneered 'nouvelle cuisine', and soon the only way anyone could be guaranteed a table at the restaurant in under three weeks was to be a film star or a Cabinet Minister.

The day Michelin gave Chez Jacques their third star Mark, with Jacques's blessing, decided to open a second restaurant. The press and customers then quarrelled amongst themselves as to which was the finer establishment. The booking sheets showed clearly the public felt there was no difference.

When in October 1986 Jacques died, at the age of seventy-one, the restaurant critics wrote confidently that standards were bound to fall. A year later the same journalists had to admit that one of the five great chefs of France had come from a town in the British Midlands they could not even pronounce.

Jacques's death only made Mark yearn more for his homeland, and when he read in the *Daily Telegraph* of a new development to be built in Covent Garden he called the site agent to ask for more details.

Mark's third restaurant was opened in the heart of London on February 11th, 1987.

* * *

Over the years Mark Hapgood often travelled back to Coventry to see his parents. His father had retired long since but Mark was still unable to persuade either parent to take the trip to Paris and sample his culinary efforts. But now he had opened in the country's capital he hoped to tempt them.

'We don't need to go up to London,' said his mother, laying the table. 'You always cook for us whenever you come home, and we read of your successes in the papers. In any case, your father isn't so good on his legs nowadays.'

'What do you call this, son?' his father asked a few minutes later as noisette of lamb surrounded by baby carrots was placed in front of him.

'*Nouvelle cuisine*.'

'And people pay good money for it?'

Mark laughed, and the following day prepared his father's favourite Lancashire hot-pot.

'Now that's a real meal,' said Arthur after his third helping. 'And I'll tell you something for nothing, lad. You cook it almost as well as your mother.'

A year later Michelin announced the restaurants throughout the world that had been awarded their coveted third star. *The Times* let its readers know on its front page that Chez Jacques was the first English restaurant ever to be so honoured.

To celebrate the award Mark's parents finally agreed to make the journey down to London, though not until Mark had sent a telegram saying he was reconsidering that job at British Leyland. He sent a car to fetch his parents and had them installed in a suite at the Savoy. That evening he reserved the most popular table at Chez Jacques in their name.

Vegetable soup followed by steak and kidney pie with a plate of bread and butter pudding to end on were not the *table d'hôte* that night, but they were served for the special guests on Table 17.

Under the influence of the finest wine, Arthur was soon chatting happily to anyone who would listen and couldn't resist reminding the head waiter that it was his son who owned the restaurant.

'Don't be silly, Arthur,' said his wife. 'He already knows that.'

'Nice couple, your parents,' the head waiter confided to his boss after he had served them with their coffee and supplied Arthur with a cigar. 'What did your old man do before he retired? Banker? Lawyer? Schoolmaster?'

'Oh no, nothing like that,' said Mark quietly.

'He spent the whole of his working life putting wheels on cars.'

'But why would he waste his time doing that?' asked the waiter incredulously.

'Because he wasn't lucky enough to have a father like mine,' Mark replied.

The Chinese Statue

The little Chinese statue was the next item to come under the auctioneer's hammer. Lot 103 caused those quiet murmurings that always precede the sale of a masterpiece. The auctioneer's assistant held up the delicate piece of ivory for the packed audience to admire while the auctioneer glanced around the room to be sure he knew where the serious bidders were seated. I studied my catalogue and read the detailed description of the piece, and what was known of its history.

The statue had been purchased in Ha Li Chuan in 1871 and was referred to as what Sotheby's quaintly described as 'the property of a gentleman', usually meaning that some member of the aristocracy did not wish to admit that he was having to sell off one of the family heirlooms. I wondered if that was the case on this occasion and decided to do some research to discover what had caused the little Chinese statue to find its way into the auction rooms on that Thursday morning over one hundred years later.

'Lot No. 103,' declared the auctioneer. 'What am I bid for this magnificent example of . . . ?'

* * *

Sir Alexander Heathcote, as well as being a gentleman, was an exact man. He was exactly six-foot-three-and-a-quarter inches tall, rose at seven o'clock every morning, joined his wife at breakfast to eat one boiled egg cooked for precisely four minutes, two pieces of toast with one spoonful of Cooper's marmalade, and drink one cup of China tea. He would then take a hackney carriage from his home in Cadogan Gardens at exactly eight-twenty and arrive at the Foreign Office at promptly eight-fifty-nine, returning home again on the stroke of six o'clock.

Sir Alexander had been exact from an early age, as became the only son of a general. But unlike his father, he chose to serve his Queen in the diplomatic service, another exacting calling. He progressed from a shared desk at the Foreign Office in Whitehall to third secretary in Calcutta, to second secretary in Vienna, to first secretary in Rome, to Deputy Ambassador in Washington, and finally to minister in Peking. He was delighted when Mr Gladstone invited him to represent the government in China as he had for some considerable time taken more than an amateur interest in the art of the Ming dynasty. This crowning appointment in his distinguished career would afford him what until then he would have considered impossible, an opportunity to observe in their natural habitat some of the great statues, paintings and drawings which he had previously been able to admire only in books.

When Sir Alexander arrived in Peking, after a journey by sea and land that took his party nearly two months, he presented his seals patent to the Empress Tzu-Hsi and a personal letter for her private reading from Queen Victoria. The Empress, dressed from head to toe in white and gold, received her new Ambassador in the throne room of the Imperial Palace. She read the letter from the British monarch while Sir Alexander remained standing to attention. Her Imperial Highness revealed nothing of its contents to the new minister, only wishing him a successful term of office in his appointment. She then moved her lips slightly up at the corners which Sir Alexander judged correctly to mean that the audience had come to an end. As he was conducted back through the great halls of the Imperial Palace by a Mandarin in the long court dress of black and gold, Sir Alexander walked as slowly as possible, taking in the magnificent collection of ivory and jade statues which were scattered casually around the building much in the way Cellini and Michelangelo today lie stacked against each other in Florence.

As his ministerial appointment was for only three years, Sir Alexander took no leave, but preferred to use his time to put the Embassy behind him and travel on horseback into the outlying districts to learn more about the country and its people. On these trips he was always accompanied by a Mandarin from the palace staff who acted as interpreter and guide.

On one such journey, passing through the muddy streets of a small village with but a few houses called Ha Li Chuan, a distance of some fifty miles from Peking, Sir Alexander chanced upon an old craftsman's working place. Leaving his servants, the minister dismounted from his horse and entered the ramshackle wooden workshop to admire the delicate pieces of ivory and jade that crammed the shelves from floor to ceiling. Although modern, the pieces were superbly executed by an experienced craftsman and the minister entered the little hut with the thought of acquiring a small memento of his journey. Once in the shop he could hardly move in any direction for fear of knocking something over. The building had not been designed for a six-foot-three-and-a-quarter visitor. Sir Alexander stood still and enthralled, taking in the fine scented jasmine smell that hung in the air.

An old craftsman bustled forward in a long, blue coolie robe and flat black hat to greet him; a jet black plaited pigtail fell down his back. He bowed very low and then looked up at the giant from England. The minister returned the bow while the Mandarin explained who Sir Alexander was and his desire to be allowed to look at the work of the craftsman. The old man was nodding his agreement even before the Mandarin had come to the end of his request. For over an hour the minister sighed and chuckled as he studied many of the pieces with admiration and finally returned to the old man to praise his skill. The craftsman bowed once again, and his shy smile revealed no teeth but only genuine pleasure at Sir Alexander's compliments. Pointing a finger to the back of the shop, he beckoned the two important visitors to follow him. They did so and entered a veritable Aladdin's Cave, with row upon row of beautiful miniature emperors and classical figures. The minister could have happily settled down in the orgy of ivory for at least a week. Sir Alexander and the craftsman chatted away to each other through the interpreter, and the minister's love and knowledge of the Ming dynasty was soon revealed. The little craftsman's face lit up with this discovery and he turned to the Mandarin and in a hushed voice made a request. The Mandarin nodded his agreement and translated.

'I have, Your Excellency, a piece of Ming myself that you might care to see. A statue that has been in my family for over seven generations.'

'I should be honoured,' said the minister.

'It is I who would be honoured, Your Excellency,' said the little man who thereupon scampered out of the back door, nearly falling over a stray dog, and on to an old peasant house a few yards behind the workshop. The minister and the Mandarin remained in the back room, for Sir Alexander knew the old man would never have considered inviting an honoured guest into his humble home until they had known each other for many years, and only then after he had been invited to Sir Alexander's home first. A few minutes passed before the little blue figure came trotting back, pigtail bouncing up and down on his shoulders. He was now clinging on to something that from the very way he held it close to his chest, had to be a treasure. The craftsman passed the piece over for the minister to study. Sir Alexander's mouth opened wide and he could not hide his excitement. The little statue, no more than six inches in height, was of the Emperor Kung and as fine an example of Ming as the minister had seen. Sir Alexander felt confident that the maker was the great Pen Q who had been patronised by the Emperor, so that the date must have been around the turn of the fifteenth century. The statue's only blemish was that the ivory base on which such pieces usually rest was missing, and a small stick protruded from the bottom of the imperial robes; but in the eyes of Sir Alexander nothing could detract from its overall beauty. Although the craftsman's lips did not move, his eyes glowed with the pleasure his guest evinced as he studied the ivory Emperor.

'You think the statue is good?' asked the craftsman through the interpreter.

'It's magnificent,' the minister replied. 'Quite magnificent.'

'My own work is not worthy to stand by its side,' added the craftsman humbly.

'No, no,' said the minister, though in truth the little craftsman knew the great man was only being kind, for Sir Alexander was holding the ivory statue in a way that already showed the same love as the old man had for the piece.

The minister smiled down at the craftsman as he handed back the Emperor Kung and then he uttered perhaps the only undiplomatic words he had ever spoken in thirty-five years of serving his Queen and country.

'How I wish the piece was mine.'

Sir Alexander regretted voicing his thoughts immediately he heard the Mandarin translate them, because he knew only too well the old Chinese tradition that if an honoured guest requests something the giver will grow in the eyes of his fellow men by parting with it.

A sad look came over the face of the little old craftsman as he handed back the figurine to the minister.

'No, no. I was only joking,' said Sir Alexander, quickly trying to return the piece to its owner.

'You would dishonour my humble home if you did not take the Emperor, Your Excellency,' the old man said anxiously and the Mandarin gravely nodded his agreement.

The minister remained silent for some time. 'I have dishonoured my own home, sir,' he replied, and looked towards the Mandarin who remained inscrutable.

The little craftsman bowed. 'I must fix a base on the statue,' he said, 'or you will not be able to put the piece on view.'

He went to a corner of the room and opened a wooden packing chest that must have housed a hundred bases for his own statues. Rummaging around he picked out a base decorated with small, dark figures that the minister did not care for but which nevertheless made a perfect fit; the old man assured Sir Alexander that although he did not know the base's history, the piece bore the mark of a good craftsman.

The embarrassed minister took the gift and tried hopelessly to thank the little old man. The craftsman once again bowed low as Sir Alexander and the expressionless Mandarin left the little workshop.

As the party travelled back to Peking, the Mandarin observed the terrible state the minister was in, and uncharacteristically spoke first:

'Your Excellency is no doubt aware,' he said, 'of the old Chinese custom that when a stranger has been generous, you must return the kindness within the calendar year.'

Sir Alexander smiled his thanks and thought carefully about the Mandarin's words. Once back in his official residence, he went immediately to the Embassy's extensive library to see if he could discover a realistic value for the little masterpiece. After much diligent research, he came across a drawing of a Ming statue that was almost an exact copy of the one now in his possession and with the help of the Mandarin he was able to assess its true worth, a figure that came to almost three years' emolument for a servant of the Crown. The minister discussed the problem with Lady Heathcote and she left her husband in no doubt as to the course of action he must take.

The following week the minister despatched a letter by private messenger to his bankers, Coutts & Co. in the Strand, London, requesting that they send a large part of his savings to reach him in Peking as quickly as possible. When the funds arrived nine weeks later the minister again approached the Mandarin, who listened to his questions and gave him the details he had asked for seven days later.

The Mandarin had discovered that the little craftsman, Yung Lee, came from the old and trusted family of Yung Shau who had for some five hundred years been craftsmen. Sir Alexander also learned that many of Yung Lee's ancestors had examples of their work in the palaces of the Manchu princes. Yung Lee himself was growing old and wished to retire to the hills above the village where his ancestors had always died. His son was ready to take over the workshop from him and continue the family tradition. The minister thanked the Mandarin for his diligence and had only one more request of him. The Mandarin listened sympathetically to the Ambassador from England and returned to the palace to seek advice.

A few days later the Empress granted Sir Alexander's request.

Almost a year to the day the minister, accompanied by the Mandarin, set out again from Peking for the village of Ha Li Chuan. When Sir Alexander arrived he immediately dismounted from his horse and entered the workshop that he remembered so well. The old man was seated at his bench, his flat hat slightly askew, a piece of uncarved ivory held lovingly between his fingers. He looked up from his work and shuffled towards the minister, not recognising his guest immediately until he could almost touch the foreign giant. Then he bowed low. The minister spoke through the Mandarin:

'I have returned, sir, within the calendar year to repay my debt.'

'There was no need, Your Excellency. My family is honoured that the little statue lives in a great Embassy and may one day be admired by the people of your own land.'

The minister could think of no words to form an adequate reply and simply requested that the old man should accompany him on a short journey.

The craftsman agreed without question and the three men set out on donkeys towards the north. They travelled for over two hours up a thin winding path into the hills behind the craftsman's workshop, and when they reached the village of Ma Tien they were met by another Mandarin, who bowed low to the minister and requested Sir Alexander and the craftsman to continue their journey with him on foot. They walked in silence to the far side of the village and only stopped when they had reached a hollow in the hill from which there was a magnificent view of the valley all the way down to Ha Li Chuan. In the hollow stood a newly completed small white house of the most perfect proportions. Two stone lion dogs, tongues hanging over their lips, guarded the front entrance. The little old craftsman who had not spoken since he had left his workshop remained mystified by the purpose of the journey until the minister turned to him and offered:

'A small, inadequate gift and my feeble attempt to repay you in kind.'

The craftsman fell to his knees and begged forgiveness of the Mandarin as he knew it was forbidden for an artisan to accept gifts from a foreigner. The Mandarin raised the frightened blue figure from the ground, explaining to his countryman that the Empress herself had sanctioned the minister's request. A smile of joy came over the face of the craftsman and he slowly walked up to the doorway of the beautiful little house, unable to resist running his hand over the carved lion dogs. The three travellers then spent over an hour admiring the little house before returning in silent mutual happiness back to the workshop in Ha Li Chuan. The two men thus parted, honour satisfied, and Sir Alexander rode to his Embassy that night content that his actions had met with the approval of the Mandarin as well as Lady Heathcote.

The minister completed his tour of duty in Peking, and the Empress awarded him the Silver Star of China and a grateful Queen added the KCVO to his already long list of decorations. After a few weeks back at the Foreign Office clearing the China desk, Sir Alexander retired to his native Yorkshire, the only English county whose inhabitants still hope to be born and die in the same place — not unlike the Chinese.

Sir Alexander spent his final years in the home of his late father with his wife and the little Ming Emperor. The statue occupied the centre of the mantelpiece in the drawing room for all to see and admire.

Being an exact man, Sir Alexander wrote a long and detailed will in which he left precise instructions for the disposal of his estate, including what was to happen to the little statue after his death. He bequeathed the Emperor Kung to his first son, requesting that he do the same, in order that the statue might always pass to the first son, or a daughter if the direct male line faltered. He also made a provision that the statue was never to be disposed of, unless the family's honour was at stake. Sir Alexander Heathcote died at the stroke of midnight in his seventieth year.

* * *

His first-born, Major James Heathcote, was serving his Queen in the Boer War at the time he came into possession of the Ming Emperor. The Major was a fighting man, commissioned with the Duke of Wellington's Regiment, and although he had little interest in culture even he could see the family heirloom was no ordinary treasure, so he loaned the statue to the regimental mess at Halifax in order that the Emperor could be displayed in the dining room for his brother officers to appreciate.

When James Heathcote became Colonel of the Dukes, the Emperor stood proudly on the table alongside the trophies won at Waterloo and Sebastopol in the Crimea and Madrid. And there the Ming statue remained until the colonel's retirement to his father's house in Yorkshire, when the Emperor returned once again to the drawing room mantelpiece. The colonel was not a man to disobey his late father, even in death, and he left clear instructions that the heirloom must always be passed on to the first-born of the Heathcotes unless the family honour was in jeopardy. Colonel James Heathcote MC did not die a soldier's death; he simply fell asleep one night by the fire, the *Yorkshire Post* on his lap.

The colonel's first-born, the Reverend Alexander Heathcote, was at the time presiding over a small flock in the parish of Much Hadham in Hertfordshire. After burying his father with military honours, he placed the little Ming Emperor on the mantelpiece of the vicarage. Few members of the Mothers' Union appreciated the masterpiece, but one or two old ladies were heard to remark on its delicate carving. And it was not until the Reverend became the Right Reverend, and the little statue found its way into the Bishop's palace, that the Emperor attracted the admiration he deserved. Many of those who visited the palace and heard the story of how the Bishop's grandfather had acquired the Ming statue were fascinated to learn of the disparity between the magnificent statue and its base. It always made a good after-dinner story.

God takes even His own ambassadors, but He did not do so before allowing Bishop Heathcote to complete a will leaving the statue to his son, with his grandfather's exact instructions carefully repeated. The Bishop's son, Captain James Heathcote, was a serving officer in his grandfather's regiment, so the Ming statue returned to the mess table in Halifax. During the Emperor's absence, the regimental trophies had been augmented by those struck for Ypres, the Marne and Verdun. The regiment was once again at war with Germany, and young Captain James Heathcote was killed on the beaches of Dunkirk and died intestate. Thereafter English law, the known wishes of his great-grandfather and common sense prevailed, and the little Emperor came into the possession of the captain's two-year-old son.

Alex Heathcote was, alas, not of the mettle of his doughty ancestors and he grew up feeling no desire to serve anyone other than himself. When Captain James had been so tragically killed, Alexander's mother lavished everything on the boy that her meagre income would allow. It didn't help, and it was not entirely young Alex's fault that he grew up to be, in the words of his grandmother, a selfish, spoiled little brat.

When Alex left school, only a short time before he would have been expelled, he found he could never hold down a job for more than a few weeks. It always seemed necessary for him to spend a little more than he, and finally his mother, could cope with. The good lady, deciding she could take no more of this life, departed it, to join all the other Heathcotes, not in Yorkshire, but in heaven.

In the swinging sixties, when casinos opened in Britain, young Alex was convinced that he had found the ideal way of earning a living without actually having to do any work. He developed a system for playing roulette with which it was impossible to lose. He did lose, so he refined the system and promptly lost more; he refined the system once again, which resulted in him having to borrow to cover his losses. Why not? If the worst came to the worst, he told himself, he could always dispose of the little Ming Emperor.

The worst did come to the worst, as each one of Alex's newly refined systems took him progressively into greater debt until the casinos began to press him for payment. When finally, one Monday morning, Alex received an unsolicited call from two gentleman who seemed determined to collect some eight thousand pounds he owed their masters, and hinted at bodily harm if the matter was not dealt with within fourteen days, Alex caved in. After all, his great-great-grandfather's instructions had been exact: the Ming statue was to be sold if the family honour was ever at stake.

Alex took the little Emperor off the mantelpiece in his Cadogan Gardens flat and stared down at its delicate handiwork, at least having the grace to feel a little sad at the loss of the family heirloom. He then drove to Bond Street and delivered the masterpiece to Sotheby's, giving instructions that the Emperor should be put up for auction.

The head of the Oriental department, a pale, thin man, appeared at the front desk to discuss the masterpiece with Alex, looking not unlike the Ming statue he was holding so lovingly in his hands.

'It will take a few days to estimate the true value of the piece,' he purred, 'but I feel confident on a cursory glance that the statue is as fine an example of Pen Q as we have ever had under the hammer.'

'That's no problem,' replied Alex, 'as long as you can let me know what it's worth within fourteen days.'

'Oh, certainly,' replied the expert. 'I feel sure I could give you a floor price by Friday.'

'Couldn't be better,' said Alex.

During that week he contacted all his creditors and without exception they were prepared to wait and learn the appraisal of the expert. Alex duly returned to Bond Street on the Friday with a large smile on his face. He knew what his great-great-grandfather had paid for the piece and felt sure that the statue must be worth more than ten thousand pounds. A sum that would not only yield him enough to cover all his debts but leave him a little over to try out his new refined, refined system on the roulette table. As he climbed the steps of Sotheby's, Alex silently thanked his great-great-grandfather. He asked the girl on reception if he could speak to the head of the Oriental department. She picked up an internal phone and the expert appeared a few moments later at the front desk with a sombre look on his face. Alex's heart sank as he listened to his words: 'A nice little piece, your Emperor, but unfortunately a fake, probably about two hundred, two hundred and fifty years old but only a copy of the original, I'm afraid. Copies were often made because . . . '

'How much is it worth?' interrupted an anxious Alex.

'Seven hundred pounds, eight hundred at the most.'

Enough to buy a gun and some bullets, thought Alex sardonically as he turned and started to walk away.

'I wonder, sir . . . ' continued the expert.

'Yes, yes, sell the bloody thing,' said Alex, without bothering to look back.

‘And what do you want me to do with the base?’

‘The base?’ repeated Alex, turning round to face the Orientalist.

‘Yes, the base. It’s quite magnificent, fifteenth century, undoubtedly a work of genius, I can’t imagine how . . . ’

⋆ ⋆ ⋆

‘Lot No. 103,’ announced the auctioneer. ‘What am I bid for this magnificent example of . . . ?’

The expert turned out to be right in his assessment. At the auction at Sotheby’s that Thursday morning I obtained the little Emperor for seven hundred and twenty guineas. And the base? That was acquired by an American gentleman of not unknown parentage for twenty-two thousand guineas.

The Wine Taster

The first occasion I met Sefton Hamilton was in late August last year when my wife and I were dining with Henry and Suzanne Kennedy at their home in Warwick Square.

Hamilton was one of those unfortunate men who have inherited immense wealth but not a lot more. He was able quickly to convince us that he had little time to read and no time to attend the theatre or opera. However, this did not prevent him from holding opinions on every subject from Shaw to Pavarotti, from Gorbachev to Picasso. He remained puzzled, for instance, as to what the unemployed had to complain about when their dole packet was only just less than what he was currently paying the labourers on his estate. In any case, they only spent it on bingo and drinking, he assured us.

Drinking brings me to the other dinner guest that night — Freddie Barker, the President of the Wine Society, who sat opposite my wife and unlike Hamilton hardly uttered a word. Henry had assured me over the phone that Barker had not only managed to get the Society back on to a proper financial footing but was also acknowledged as a leading authority on his subject. I looked forward to picking up useful bits of inside knowledge. Whenever Barker was allowed to get a word in edgeways, he showed enough knowledge of the topic under discussion to convince me that he would be fascinating if only Hamilton would remain silent long enough for him to speak.

While our hostess produced as a starter a spinach soufflé that melted in the mouth, Henry moved round the table pouring each of us a glass of wine.

Barker sniffed his appreciatively. 'Appropriate in bicentennial year that we should be drinking an Australian Chablis of such fine vintage. I feel sure their whites will soon be making the French look to their laurels.'

'Australian?' said Hamilton in disbelief as he put down his glass. 'How could a nation of beerswiggers begin to understand the first thing about producing a half decent wine?'

'I think you'll find,' began Barker, 'that the Australians — '

'Bicentennial indeed,' Hamilton continued. 'Let's face it, they're only celebrating two hundred years of parole.' No one laughed except Hamilton. 'I'd still pack the rest of our criminals off there, given half a chance.'

No one doubted him.

Hamilton sipped the wine tentatively, like a man who fears he is about to be poisoned, then began to explain why, in his considered view, judges were far too lenient with petty criminals. I found myself concentrating more on the food than the incessant flow of my neighbour's views.

I always enjoy Beef Wellington, and Suzanne can produce a pastry that doesn't flake when cut and meat that's so tender that once one has finished a first helping, Oliver Twist comes to mind. It certainly helped me to endure Hamilton's pontificating. Barker managed to pass an appreciative comment to Henry on the quality of the claret between Hamilton's opinions on the chances of Paddy Ashdown reviving the Liberal Party and the role of Arthur Scargill in the trade union movement, allowing no one the chance to reply.

'I don't allow my staff to belong to any union,' Hamilton declared, gulping down his drink. 'I run a closed shop.' He laughed once more at his own joke and held his empty glass high in the air as if it would be filled by magic. In fact it was filled by Henry with a discretion that shamed Hamilton — not that he noticed. In the brief pause that followed, my wife suggested that perhaps the trade union movement had been born out of a response to a genuine social need.

'Balderdash, madam,' said Hamilton. 'With great respect, the trade unions have been the single most important factor in the decline of Britain as we know it. They've no interest in anybody but themselves. You only have to look at Ron Todd and the whole Ford fiasco to understand that.'

Suzanne began to clear the plates away, and I noticed she took the opportunity to nudge Henry, who quickly changed the subject.

Moments later a raspberry meringue glazed with a thick sauce appeared. It seemed a pity to cut such a creation but Suzanne carefully divided six generous helpings like a nanny feeding her charges while Henry uncorked a

1981 Sauternes. Barker literally licked his lips in anticipation.

'And another thing,' Hamilton was saying. 'The Prime Minister has got far too many Wets in her Cabinet for my liking.'

'With whom would you replace them?' asked Barker innocently.

Herod would have had little trouble in convincing the list of gentleman Hamilton proffered that the slaughter of the innocents was merely an extension of the child care programme.

Once again I became more interested in Suzanne's culinary efforts, especially as she had allowed me an indulgence: Cheddar was to be served as the final course. I knew the moment I tasted it that it had been purchased from the Alvis Brothers' farm in Keynsham; we all have to be knowledgeable about something, and Cheddar is my speciality.

To accompany the cheese, Henry supplied a port which was to be the highlight of the evening. 'Sandeman 1970,' he said in an aside to Barker as he poured the first drops into the expert's glass.

'Yes, of course,' said Barker, holding it to his nose. 'I would have known it anywhere. Typical Sandeman warmth but with real body. I hope you've laid some down, Henry,' he added. 'You'll enjoy it even more in your old age.'

'Think you're a bit of an authority on wines, do you?' said Hamilton, the first question he had asked all evening.

'Not exactly,' began Barker, 'but I — '

'You're all a bunch of humbugs, the lot of you,' interrupted Hamilton. 'You sniff and you swirl, you taste and you spit, then you spout a whole lot of gobbledegook and expect us to swallow it. Body and warmth be damned. You can't take me in that easily.'

'No one was trying to,' said Barker with feeling.

'You've been keen to put one over on us all evening,' replied Hamilton, 'with your 'Yes, of course, I'd have known it anywhere' routine. Come on, admit it.'

'I didn't mean to suggest — ' added Barker.

'I'll prove it, if you like,' said Hamilton.

The five of us stared at the ungracious guest and, for the first time that evening, I wondered what could possibly be coming next.

'I have heard it said,' continued Hamilton, 'that Sefton Hall boasts one of the finest wine cellars in England. It was laid down by my father and his father before him, though I confess I haven't found the time to continue the tradition.' Barker nodded in belief. 'But my butler knows exactly what I like. I therefore invite you, sir, to join me for lunch on the Saturday after next, when I will produce four wines of the finest vintage for your consideration. And I offer you a wager,' he added, looking straight at Barker. 'Five hundred pounds to fifty a bottle — tempting odds, I'm sure you'll agree — that you will be unable to name any one of them.' He stared belligerently at the distinguished President of the Wine Society.

'The sum is so large that I could not consider — '

'Unwilling to take up the challenge, eh, Barker? Then you are, sir, a coward as well as a humbug.'

After the embarrassing pause that followed, Barker replied, 'As you wish, sir. It appears I am left with no choice but to accept your challenge.'

A satisfied grin appeared on the other man's face. 'You must come along as a witness, Henry,' he said, turning to our host. 'And why don't you bring along that author johnny?' he added, pointing at me. 'Then he'll really have something to write about for a change.'

From Hamilton's manner it was obvious that the feelings of our wives were not to be taken into consideration. Mary gave me a wry smile.

Henry looked anxiously towards me, but I was quite content to be an observer of this unfolding drama. I nodded my assent.

'Good,' said Hamilton, rising from his place, his napkin still tucked under his collar. 'I look forward to seeing the three of you at Sefton Hall on Saturday week. Shall we say twelve-thirty?' He bowed to Suzanne.

'I won't be able to join you, I'm afraid,' she said, clearing up any lingering doubt she might have been included in the invitation. 'I always have lunch with my mother on Saturdays.'

Hamilton waved a hand to signify that it did not concern him one way or the other.

After the strange guest had left we sat in silence for some moments before Henry volunteered a statement. 'I'm sorry about all that,' he began. 'His mother and my aunt are old friends and she's asked me on several occasions to have him over to dinner. It seems no one else will.'

'Don't worry,' said Barker eventually. 'I'll do my best not to let you down. And in return for such excellent hospitality perhaps both of you would be kind enough to leave Saturday evening free? There is,' he explained, 'an inn near Sefton Hall I have wanted to visit for some time: the Hamilton Arms. The food, I'm assured, is more than adequate but the wine list is . . . ' he hesitated, 'considered by experts to be exceptional.'

Henry and I both checked our diaries and readily accepted his invitation.

* * *

I thought a great deal about Sefton Hamilton during the next ten days and awaited our lunch with a mixture of apprehension and anticipation. On the Saturday morning Henry drove the three of us down to Sefton Park and we arrived a little after twelve-thirty. Actually we passed through the massive wrought-iron gates at twelve-thirty precisely, but did not reach the front door of the house until twelve-thirty-seven.

The great oak door was opened before we had a chance to knock by a tall elegant man in a tail coat, wing collar and black tie. He informed us that he was Adams, the butler. He then escorted us to the morning room, where we were greeted by a large log fire.

Above it hung a picture of a disapproving man who I presumed was Sefton Hamilton's grandfather. On the other walls were a massive tapestry of the Battle of Waterloo and an enormous oil of the Crimean War. Antique furniture littered the room and the one sculpture on display was of a Greek figure throwing a discus. Looking around, I reflected that only the telephone belonged to the present century.

Sefton Hamilton entered the room as a gale might hit an unhappy seaside town. Immediately he stood with his back to the fire, blocking any heat we might have been appreciating.

'Whisky!' he bellowed as Adams appeared once again. 'Barker?'

'Not for me,' said Barker with a thin smile.

'Ah,' said Hamilton. 'Want to keep your taste buds at their most sensitive, eh?'

Barker did not reply. Before we went into lunch we learned that the estate was seven thousand acres in size and had some of the finest shooting outside of Scotland. The Hall had one hundred and twelve rooms, one or two of which Hamilton had not visited since he was a child. The roof itself, he assured us finally, was an acre and a half, a statistic that will long remain in my memory as it is the same size as my garden.

The long-case clock in the corner of the room struck one. 'Time for the contest to begin,' declared Hamilton, and marched out of the room like a general who assumes his troops will follow him without question. We did, all the way down thirty yards of corridor to the dining room. The four of us then took our places around a seventeenth-century oak table that could comfortably have seated twenty.

Adorning the centre of the table were two Georgian decanters and two unlabelled bottles. The first bottle was filled with a clear white wine, the first decanter with a red, the second bottle with a richer white and the second decanter with a tawny red substance. In front of the four wines were four white cards. By each lay a slim bundle of fifty-pound notes.

Hamilton took his place in the large chair at the top of the table while Barker and I sat opposite each other in the centre, facing the wine, leaving Henry to occupy the final place at the far end of the table.

The butler stood one pace behind his master's chair. He nodded and four footmen appeared, bearing the first course. A fish and prawn terrine was placed in front of each of us. Adams received a nod from his master before he picked up the first bottle and began to fill Barker's glass. Barker waited for the butler to go round the table and fill the other three glasses before he began his ritual.

First he swirled the wine round while at the same time studying it carefully. Then he sniffed it. He hesitated and a surprised look came over his face. He took a sip.

'Um,' he said eventually. 'I confess, quite a challenge.' He sniffed it again just to be sure. Then he looked up and gave a smile of satisfaction. Hamilton stared at him, his mouth slightly open, although he remained unusually silent.

Barker took one more sip. 'Montagny Tête de Cuvée 1985,' he declared with the confidence of an expert, 'bottled by Louis Latour.' We all looked towards Hamilton who, in contrast, displayed an unhappy frown.

'You're right,' said Hamilton. 'It was bottled by Latour. But that's about as clever as telling us that Heinz bottle tomato sauce. And as my father died in 1984 I can assure you, sir, you are mistaken.' He looked round at his butler to confirm the statement. Adams's face remained inscrutable. Barker turned over the card. It read: 'Chevalier Montrachet Les Demorselles 1983'. He stared at the card, obviously unable to believe his eyes.

'One down and three to go,' Hamilton declared, oblivious to Barker's reaction. The footmen reappeared and took away the fish plates, to replace them a few moments later with lightly cooked grouse. While its accompaniments were being served Barker did not speak. He just stared at the other three decanters, not even hearing his host inform Henry who his guests were to be for the first shoot of the season the following week. I remember that the names corresponded roughly with the ones Hamilton had suggested for his ideal Cabinet.

Barker nibbled at the grouse as he waited for Adams to fill a glass from the first decanter. He had not finished his terrine after the opening failure, only taking the occasional sip of water.

'As Adams and I spent a considerable part of

our morning selecting the wines for this little challenge, let us hope you can do better this time,' said Hamilton, unable to hide his satisfaction. Barker once again began to swirl the wine round. He seemed to take longer this time, sniffing it several times before putting his glass to his lips and finally sipping from it.

A smile of instant recognition appeared on his face and he did not hesitate. 'Château la Louvière 1978.'

'This time you have the correct year, sir, but you have insulted the wine.'

Immediately Barker turned the card over and read it out incredulously: Château Lafite 1978. Even I knew that to be one of the finest clarets one might ever hope to taste. Barker lapsed into a deep silence and continued to nibble at his food. Hamilton appeared to be enjoying the wine almost as much as the half-time score. 'One hundred pounds to me, nothing to the President of the Wine Society,' he reminded us. Embarrassed, Henry and I tried to keep the conversation going until the third course had been served — a lemon and lime soufflé which could not compare in presentation or subtlety with any of Suzanne's offerings.

'Shall we move on to my third challenge?' asked Hamilton crisply.

Once again, Adams picked up a decanter and began to pour the wine. I was surprised to see that he spilled a little as he filled Barker's glass.

'Clumsy oaf,' barked Hamilton.

'I do apologise, sir,' said Adams. He removed the spilled drop from the wooden table with a napkin. As he did so he stared at Barker with a desperate look that I felt sure had nothing to do with the spilling of the wine. However, he remained mute as he continued to circle the table.

Once again Barker went through his ritual, the swirling, the sniffing and finally the tasting. This time he took even longer. Hamilton became impatient and drummed the great Jacobean table with his podgy fingers.

'It's a Sauternes,' began Barker.

'Any half-wit could tell you that,' said Hamilton. 'I want to know the year and the vintage.'

His guest hesitated.

'Château Guiraud 1976,' he said flatly.

'At least you are consistent,' said Hamilton. 'You're always wrong.'

Barker flicked over the card.

'Château d'Yquem 1980,' he said in disbelief. It was a vintage that I had only seen at the bottom of wine lists in expensive restaurants and had never had the privilege of tasting. It puzzled me greatly that Barker could have been wrong about the Mona Lisa of wines.

Barker quickly turned towards Hamilton to protest and must have seen Adams standing behind his master, all six-foot-three of the man trembling, at exactly the same time I did. I wanted Hamilton to leave the room so I could ask Adams what was making him so fearful, but the owner of Sefton Hall was now in full cry.

Meanwhile Barker gazed at the butler for a moment more and, sensing his discomfort, lowered his eyes and contributed nothing else to the conversation until the port was poured some twenty minutes later.

'Your last chance to avoid complete humiliation,' said Hamilton.

A cheese board, displaying several varieties, was brought round and each guest selected his choice — I stuck to a Cheddar that I could have told Hamilton had not been made in Somerset. Meanwhile the port was poured by the butler, who was now as white as a sheet. I began to wonder if he was going to faint, but somehow he managed to fill all four glasses before returning to stand a pace behind his master's chair. Hamilton noticed nothing untoward.

Barker drank the port, not bothering with any of his previous preliminaries.

'Taylor's,' he began.

'Agreed,' said Hamilton. 'But as there are only three decent suppliers of port in the world, the year can be all that matters — as you, in your exalted position, must be well aware, Mr Barker.'

Freddie nodded his agreement. 'Nineteen seventy-five,' he said firmly, then quickly flicked the card over.

'Taylor's 1927', I read upside-down.

Once again Barker turned sharply towards his host, who was rocking with laughter. The butler stared back at his master's guest with haunted eyes. Barker hesitated only for a moment before removing a chequebook from his inside pocket. He filled in the name 'Sefton Hamilton' and the figure of £200. He signed it and wordlessly passed the cheque along the table to his host.

'That was only half the bargain,' said Hamilton, enjoying every moment of his triumph.

Barker rose, paused and said, 'I am a humbug.'

'You are indeed, sir,' said Hamilton.

After spending three of the most unpleasant hours of my life, I managed to escape with Henry and Freddie Barker a little after four o'clock. As Henry drove away from Sefton Hall neither of us uttered a word. Perhaps we both felt that Barker should be allowed the first comment.

'I fear, gentlemen,' he said eventually, 'I shall not be good company for the next few hours, and so I will, with your permission, take a brisk walk and join you both for dinner at the Hamilton Arms around seven-thirty. I have booked a table for eight o'clock.' Without another word, Barker signalled that Henry should bring the car to a halt and we watched as he climbed out and headed off down a country lane. Henry did not drive on until his friend was well out of sight.

My sympathies were entirely with Barker, although I remained puzzled by the whole affair. How could the President of the Wine Society make such basic mistakes? After all, I could read one page of Dickens and know it wasn't Graham Greene.

Like Dr Watson, I felt I required a fuller explanation.

* * *

Barker found us sitting round the fire in the private bar at the Hamilton Arms a little after seven-thirty that night. Following his exercise, he appeared in far better spirits. He chatted about nothing consequential and didn't once mention what had taken place at lunchtime.

It must have been a few minutes later, when I turned to check the old clock above the door, that I saw Hamilton's butler seated at the bar in earnest conversation with the innkeeper. I would have thought nothing of it had I not noticed the same terrified look that I had witnessed earlier in the afternoon as he pointed in our direction. The innkeeper appeared equally anxious, as if he had been found guilty of serving half-measures by a customs and excise officer.

He picked up some menus and walked over to our table.

'We've no need for those,' said Barker. 'Your reputation goes before you. We are in your hands. Whatever you suggest we will happily consume.'

'Thank you, sir,' he said and passed our host the wine list.

Barker studied the contents inside the leatherbound covers for some time before a large smile appeared on his face. 'I think you had better select the wines as well,' he said, 'as I have a feeling you know the sort of thing I would expect.'

'Of course, sir,' said the innkeeper as Freddie passed back the wine list, leaving me totally mystified, remembering that this was Barker's first visit to the inn.

The innkeeper left for the kitchens while we chatted away and didn't reappear for some fifteen minutes.

'Your table is ready, gentlemen,' he said, and we followed him into an adjoining dining room. There were only a dozen tables, and as ours was the last to be filled there was no doubting the inn's popularity.

The innkeeper had selected a light supper of consommé, followed by thin slices of duck, almost as if he had known that we would be unable to handle another heavy meal after our lunch at the Hall.

I was also surprised to find that all the wines he had chosen were served in decanters, and I assumed that the innkeeper must therefore have selected the house wines. As each was poured and consumed I admit that, to my untutored palate, they seemed far superior to those I had drunk at Sefton Hall earlier that day. Barker certainly seemed to linger over every mouthful and on one occasion said appreciatively, 'This is the real McCoy.'

At the end of the evening when our table had been cleared we sat back and enjoyed a magnificent port and smoked cigars.

It was at this point that Henry mentioned Hamilton for the first time.

'Are you going to let us into the mystery of what really happened at lunch today?' he asked.

'I'm still not altogether sure myself,' came back Barker's reply, 'but I am certain of one thing: Mr Hamilton's father was a man who knew his wines, while his son doesn't.'

I would have pressed Barker further on the subject if the innkeeper had not arrived by his side at that moment.

'An excellent meal,' Barker declared. 'And as for the wine — quite exceptional.'

'You are kind, sir,' said the innkeeper, as he handed him the bill.

My curiosity got the better of me, I'm sorry to admit, and I glanced at the bottom of the slim strip of paper. I couldn't believe my eyes — the bill came to two hundred pounds.

To my surprise, Barker only commented, 'Very reasonable, considering.' He wrote out a cheque and passed it over to the innkeeper. 'I have only tasted Château d'Yquem 1980 once before today,' he added, 'and Taylor's 1927 never.'

The innkeeper smiled. 'I hope you enjoyed them both, sir. I feel sure you wouldn't have wanted to see them wasted on a humbug.'

Barker nodded his agreement.

I watched as the innkeeper left the dining room and returned to his place behind the bar.

He passed the cheque over to Adams the butler, who studied it for a moment, smiled and then tore it into little pieces.

Not The Real Thing

Gerald Haskins and Walter Ramsbottom had been eating cornflakes for over a year.

'I'll swap you my MC and DSO for your VC,' said Walter, on the way to school one morning.

'Never,' said Gerald. 'In any case, it takes ten packet tops to get a VC and you only need two for an MC or a DSO.'

Gerald went on collecting packet tops until he had every medal displayed on the back of the packet.

Walter never got the VC.

Angela Bradbury thought they were both silly.

'They're only replicas,' she continually reminded them, 'not the real thing. And *I* am only interested in the real thing,' she told them haughtily.

Neither Gerald nor Walter cared for Angela's opinion at the time, both boys still being more interested in medals than the views of the opposite sex.

Kellogg's offer of free medals ended on 1 January 1950, just at the time when Gerald had managed to complete the set.

Walter gave up eating cornflakes.

Children of the fifties were then given the opportunity to discover the world of Meccano. Meccano demanded eating even more cornflakes, and within a year Gerald had collected a large enough set to build bridges, pontoons, cranes and even an office block.

Gerald's family nobly went on munching cornflakes, but when he told them he wanted to build a whole town — Kellogg's positively final offer — it took nearly all his friends in the fifth form at Hull Grammar School to assist him in consuming enough breakfast cereal to complete his ambition.

Walter Ramsbottom refused to be of assistance.

Angela Bradbury's help was never sought.

All three continued on their separate ways.

Two years later, when Gerald Haskins won a place at Durham University, no one was surprised that he chose to read engineering and listed as his main hobby collecting medals.

Walter Ramsbottom joined his father in the family jewellery business and started courting Angela Bradbury.

It was during the spring holiday in Gerald's second year at Durham that he came across Walter and Angela again. They were sitting in the same row at a Bach cello concert in Hull Town Hall. Walter told him in the interval that they had just become engaged but had not yet settled on a date for the wedding.

Gerald hadn't seen Angela for over a year, but this time he did listen to her opinions, because like Walter he fell in love with her.

He replaced eating cornflakes with continually inviting Angela out to dinner in an effort to win her away from his old rival.

Gerald notched up another victory when Angela returned her engagement ring to Walter a few days before Christmas.

Walter spread it around that Gerald only wanted to marry Angela because her father was chairman of the Hull City Amenities Committee and he was hoping to get a job with the council after he'd taken his degree at Durham. When the invitations for the wedding were sent out, Walter was not on the guest list.

* * *

Mr and Mrs Haskins travelled to Multavia for their honeymoon, partly because they couldn't afford Nice and didn't want to go to Cleethorpes. In any case, the local travel agent was making a special offer for those considering a visit to the tiny kingdom sandwiched between Austria and Czechoslovakia.

When the newly married couple arrived at their hotel in Teske, the capital, they discovered why the terms had been so reasonable.

Multavia was, in 1959, going through an identity crisis as it attempted to adjust to yet another treaty drawn up by a Dutch lawyer in Geneva, written in French, but with the Russians and Americans in mind. However, thanks to King Alfons III, their shrewd and popular monarch, the kingdom continued to enjoy uninterrupted grants from the West and non-disruptive visits from the East.

The capital of Multavia, the Haskins were quickly to discover, had an average temperature of 92°F in June, no rainfall and the remains of a sewerage system that had been indiscriminately bombed by both sides between 1939 and 1944. Angela actually found herself holding her nose as she walked through the cobbled streets. The People's Hotel claimed to have forty-five rooms, but what the brochure did not point out was that only three of them had bathrooms and none of those had bath plugs. Then there was the food, or lack of it; for the first time in his life Gerald lost weight.

The honeymoon couple were also to discover that Multavia boasted no monuments, art galleries, theatres or opera houses worthy of the name, and that the outlying country was flatter and less interesting than the fens of Cambridgeshire. The kingdom had no coastline and the only river, the Plotz, flowed from Germany and on into Russia, thus ensuring that none of the locals trusted it.

By the end of their honeymoon the Haskins were only too pleased to find that Multavia did not boast a national airline. BOAC got them home safely, and that would have been the end of Gerald's experience of Multavia had it not been for those sewers — or the lack of them.

* * *

Once the Haskins had returned to Hull, Gerald took up his appointment as an assistant in the engineering department of the city council. His first job was as a third engineer with special responsibility for the city's sewerage. Most ambitious young men would have treated such an appointment as nothing more than a step on life's ladder. Gerald however did not. He quickly made contact with all the leading sewerage companies, their advisers and his opposite numbers throughout the county.

Two years later he was able to put in front of his father-in-law's committee a paper showing how the council could save a considerable amount of the ratepayers' money by redeveloping its sewerage system.

The committee were impressed and decided to carry out Mr Haskins's recommendation, and at the same time appointed him second engineer.

That was the first occasion Walter Ramsbottom stood for the council; he wasn't elected.

When, three years later, the network of little tunnels and waterways had been completed, Gerald's diligence was rewarded by his appointment as deputy borough engineer. In the same year his father-in-law became Mayor and Walter Ramsbottom became a councillor.

Councils up and down the country were now acknowledging Gerald as a man whose opinion should be sought if they had any anxieties about their sewerage system. This provoked an irreverent round of jokes at every Rotary Club dinner Gerald attended, but they nevertheless still hailed him as the leading authority in his field, or drain.

When in 1966 the Borough of Halifax considered putting out to tender the building of a new sewerage system they first consulted Gerald Haskins — Yorkshire being the one place on earth where a prophet is with honour in his own country.

After spending a day in Halifax with the town council's senior engineer and realising how much had to be spent on the new system, Gerald remarked to his wife, not for the first time, 'Where there's muck there's brass.' But it was Angela who was shrewd enough to work out just how much of that brass her husband could get hold of with the minimum of risk. During the next few days Gerald considered his wife's proposition and when he returned to Halifax the following week it was not to visit the council chambers but the Midland Bank. Gerald did not select the Midland by chance; the manager of the bank was also chairman of the planning committee on the Halifax borough council.

A deal that suited both sides was struck between the two Yorkshiremen, and with the bank's blessing Gerald resigned his position as deputy borough engineer and formed a private company. When he presented his tender, in competition with several large organisations from London, no one was surprised that Haskins of Hull was selected unanimously by the planning committee to carry out the job.

Three years later Halifax had a fine new sewerage system and the Midland Bank was delighted to be holding Haskins of Hull's company account.

Over the next fifteen years Chester, Runcorn, Huddersfield, Darlington, Macclesfield and York were jointly and severally grateful for the services rendered to them by Gerald Haskins, of Haskins & Co plc.

Haskins & Co (International) plc then began

contract work in Dubai, Lagos and Rio de Janeiro. In 1983 Gerald received the Queen's Award for Industry from a grateful government, and a year later he was made a Commander of the British Empire by a grateful monarch.

The investiture took place at Buckingham Palace in the same year as King Alfons III of Multavia died and was succeeded by his son King Alfons IV. The newly crowned King decided something had finally to be done about the drainage problems of Teske. It had been his father's dying wish that his people should not go on suffering those unseemly smells, and King Alfons IV did not intend to bequeath the problem to *his* son.

After much begging and borrowing from the West, and much visiting and talking with the East, the newly anointed monarch decided to invite tenders for a new sewerage system in the kingdom's capital.

The tender document supplying several pages of details and listing the problems facing any engineer who wished to tackle the problem arrived with a thud on most of the boardroom tables of the world's major engineering companies. Once the paperwork had been seriously scrutinised and the realistic opportunity for a profit considered, King Alfons IV received only a few replies. Nevertheless, the King was able to sit up all night considering the merits of the three interested companies that had been shortlisted. Kings are also human, and when Alfons discovered that Gerald had chosen Multavia for his honeymoon some twenty-five years before it tipped the balance. By the time Alfons IV fell asleep that morning he had decided to accept Haskins & Co (International) plc's tender.

And thus Gerald Haskins made his second visit to Multavia, this time accompanied by a site manager, three draughtsmen and eleven engineers. Gerald had a private audience with the King and assured him the job would be completed on time and for the price specified. He also told the King how much he was enjoying his second visit to his country. However, when he returned to England he assured his wife that there was still little in Multavia that could be described as entertainment before or after the hour of seven.

* * *

A few years later, and after some considerable haggling over the increase in the cost of materials, Teske ended up with one of the finest sewerage systems in Central Europe. The King was delighted — although he continued to grumble about how Haskins & Co had over-run the original contract price. The words 'contingency payment' had to be explained to the monarch several times, who realised that the extra two hundred and forty thousand pounds would in turn have to be explained to the East and 'borrowed' from the West. After many veiled threats and 'without prejudice' solicitors' letters, Haskins & Co received the final payment, but not until the King had been given a further grant from the British government, a payment which involved the Midland Bank, Sloane Street, transferring a sum of money to the Midland Bank, High Street, Hull, without Multavia ever getting their hands on it. This was after all, Gerald explained to his wife, how most overseas aid was distributed.

* * *

Thus the story of Gerald Haskins and the drainage problems of Teske might have ended, had not the British Foreign Secretary decided to pay a visit to the kingdom of Multavia.

The original purpose of the Foreign Secretary's European trip was to take in Warsaw and Prague, in order to see how *glasnost* and *perestroika* were working in those countries. But when the Foreign Office discovered how much aid had been allocated to Multavia, and after they explained to their minister its role as a buffer state, the Foreign Secretary decided to accept King Alfons's longstanding invitation to visit the tiny kingdom. Such excursions to smaller countries by British Foreign Secretaries usually take place in airport lounges, a habit the British picked up from Henry Kissinger, and later Comrade Gorbachev; but not on this occasion. It was felt Multavia warranted a full day.

As the hotels had improved only slightly since the time of Gerald's honeymoon, the Foreign Secretary was invited to lodge at the palace. He was asked by the King to undertake only two official engagements during his brief stay: the opening of the capital's new sewerage system, and a formal banquet.

Once the Foreign Secretary had agreed to these requests the King invited Gerald and his wife to be present at the opening ceremony — at their own expense. When the day of the opening came the Foreign Secretary delivered the appropriate speech for the occasion. He first praised Gerald Haskins for a remarkable piece of work in the great tradition of British engineering, then commended Multavia for her shrewd common sense in awarding the contract to a British company in the first place. The Foreign Secretary omitted to mention the fact that the British government had ended up underwriting the entire project. Gerald, however, was touched by the minister's words, and said as much to the Foreign Secretary after the latter had pulled the lever that opened the first sluice gate.

That evening in the palace there was a banquet for over three hundred guests, including the ambassadorial corps and several leading British businessmen. There followed the usual interminable speeches about 'historic links', Multavia's role in Anglo — Soviet affairs and the 'special relationship' with Britain's own royal family.

The highlight of the evening, however, came after the speeches, when the King made two investitures. The first was the award of the Order of the Peacock (Second Class) to the Foreign Secretary. 'The highest award a commoner can receive,' the King explained to the assembled audience, 'as the Order of the Peacock (First

Class) is reserved for royalty and heads of state.'

The King then announced a second investiture. The Order of the Peacock (Third Class) was to be awarded to Gerald Haskins, CBE, for his work on the drainage system of Teske. Gerald was surprised and delighted as he was conducted from his place on the top table to join the King, who leaned forward to put a large gold chain encrusted with gems of various colours and sizes over his visitor's head. Gerald took two respectful paces backwards and bowed low, as the Foreign Secretary looked up from his seat and smiled encouragingly at him.

Gerald was the last foreign guest to leave the banquet that night. Angela, who had left on her own over two hours before, had already fallen asleep by the time he returned to their hotel room. He placed the chain on the bed, undressed, put on his pyjamas, checked his wife was still asleep and then placed the chain back over his head to rest on his shoulders.

Gerald stood and looked at himself in the bathroom mirror for several minutes. He could not wait to return home.

The moment Gerald got back to Hull he dictated a letter to the Foreign Office. He requested permission to be allowed to wear his new award on those occasions when it stipulated on the bottom right-hand corner of invitation cards that decorations and medals should be worn. The Foreign Office duly referred the matter to the Palace, where the Queen, a distant cousin of King Alfons IV, agreed to the request.

The next official occasion at which Gerald was

given the opportunity to sport the Order of the Peacock was the Mayor-making ceremony held in the chamber of Hull's City Hall, which was to be preceded by dinner at the Guildhall.

Gerald returned especially from Lagos for the occasion, and even before changing into his dinner jacket couldn't resist a glance at the Order of the Peacock (Third Class). He opened the box that held his prize possession and stared down in disbelief: the gold had become tarnished, and one of the stones looked as if it was coming loose. Mrs Haskins stopped dressing in order to steal a glance at the order. 'It's not gold,' she declared with a simplicity that would have stopped the IMF in their tracks.

Gerald offered no comment and quickly fixed the loose stone back in place with Araldite, but he had to admit to himself that the craftmanship didn't bear careful scrutiny. Neither of them mentioned the subject again on their journey to Hull's City Hall.

Some of the guests during the Mayor's dinner that night at the Guildhall enquired after the history of the Order of the Peacock (Third Class), and although it gave Gerald some considerable satisfaction to explain how he had come by the distinction and indeed the Queen's permission to wear it on official occasions, he felt one or two of his colleagues had been less than awed by the tarnished peacock. Gerald also considered it was somewhat unfortunate that they had ended up on the same table as Walter Ramsbottom, now the Deputy Mayor.

'I suppose it would be hard to put a true value

on it,' said Walter, staring disdainfully at the chain.

'It certainly would,' said Gerald firmly.

'I didn't mean a monetary value,' said the jeweller with a smirk. 'That would be only too easy to ascertain. I meant a sentimental value, of course.'

'Of course,' said Gerald. 'And are you expecting to be the Mayor next year?' he asked, trying to change the subject.

'It is the tradition,' said Walter, 'that the Deputy succeeds the Mayor if he doesn't serve for a second year. And be assured, Gerald, that I shall see to it that you are placed on the top table for that occasion.' Walter paused. 'The Mayor's chain, you know, is fourteen-carat gold.'

Gerald left the banquet early that evening, determined to do something about the Order of the Peacock before it was Walter's turn to be Mayor.

None of Gerald's friends would have described him as an extravagant man, and even his wife was surprised at the whim of vanity that was to follow. At nine o'clock the next morning Gerald rang his office to say he would not be in to work that day. He then travelled by train to London, to visit Bond Street in general and a famed jeweller in particular.

The door of the Bond Street shop was opened for Gerald by a sergeant from the Corps of Commissionaires. Once he had stepped inside Gerald explained his problem to the tall, thin gentleman in a black suit who had come forward to welcome him. He was then led to a circular glass counter in the middle of the shop floor.

'Our Mr Pullinger will be with you in a moment,' he was assured. Moments later Asprey's fine-gems expert arrived and happily agreed to Gerald's request to value the Order of the Peacock (Third Class). Mr Pullinger placed the chain on a black velvet cushion before closely studying the stones through a small eyeglass.

After a cursory glance he frowned with the disappointment of a man who has won third prize at a shooting range on Blackpool pier.

'So, what's it worth?' asked Gerald bluntly after several minutes had elapsed.

'Hard to put a value on something so intricately' — Pullinger hesitated — 'unusual.'

'The stones are glass and the gold's brass, that's what you're trying to say, isn't it, lad?'

Mr Pullinger gave a look that indicated that he could not have put it more succinctly himself.

'You might possibly be able to get a few hundred pounds from someone who collects such objects, but . . . '

'Oh, no,' said Gerald, quite offended. 'I have no interest in selling it. My purpose in coming up to London was to find out if you can *copy* it.'

'Copy it?' said the expert in disbelief.

'Aye,' said Gerald. 'First, I want every stone to be the correct gem according to its colour. Second, I expect a setting that would impress a duchess. And third, I require the finest craftsman put to work on it in nothing less than eighteen-carat gold.'

The expert from Asprey's, despite years of

dealing with Arab clients, was unable to conceal his surprise.

'It would not be cheap,' he uttered *sotto voce*: the word 'cheap' was one of which Asprey's clearly disapproved.

'I never doubted that for one moment,' said Gerald. 'But you must understand that this is a once-in-a-lifetime honour for me. Now, when could I hope to have an estimate?'

'A month, six weeks at the most,' replied the expert.

Gerald left the plush carpet of Asprey's for the sewers of Nigeria. When a little over a month later he flew back to London, he travelled in to the West End for his second meeting with Mr Pullinger.

The jeweller had not forgotten Gerald Haskins and his strange request, and he quickly produced from his order book a neatly folded piece of paper. Gerald unfolded it and read the tender slowly. Requirement for customer's request: twelve diamonds, seven amethysts, three rubies and a sapphire, all to be of the most perfect colour and of the highest quality. A peacock to be sculpted in ivory and painted by a craftsman. The entire chain then to be moulded in the finest eighteen-carat gold. The bottom line read: 'Two hundred and eleven thousand pounds — exclusive of VAT.'

Gerald, who would have thought nothing of haggling over an estimate of a few thousand pounds for roofing material or the hire of heavy equipment, or even a schedule of payments, simply asked, 'When will I be able to collect it?'

'One could not be certain how long it might take to put together such a fine piece,' said Mr Pullinger. 'Finding stones of a perfect match and colour will, I fear, take a little time.' He paused. 'I am also hoping that our senior craftsman will be free to work on this particular commission. He has been rather taken up lately with gifts for the Queen's forthcoming visit to Saudi Arabia, so I don't think it could be ready before the end of March.'

Well in time for next year's Mayor's banquet, thought Gerald. Councillor Ramsbottom would not be able to mock him this time. Fourteen-carat gold, had he said?

* * *

Lagos and Rio de Janeiro both had their sewers down and running long before Gerald was able to return to Asprey's. And he only set his eyes on the unique prize a few weeks before Mayor-making day.

When Mr Pullinger first showed his client the finished work the Yorkshireman gasped with delight. The Order was so magnificent that Gerald found it necessary to purchase a string of pearls from Asprey's to ensure a silent wife.

On his return to Hull he waited until after dinner to open the green leather box from Asprey's and surprise her with the new Order. 'Fit for a monarch, lass,' he assured his wife, but Angela seemed preoccupied with her pearls.

After Angela had left to wash up, her husband continued to stare for some time at the beautiful jewels so expertly crafted and superbly cut before he finally closed the box. The next morning he reluctantly took the piece round to the bank and explained that it must be kept safely locked in the vaults, as he would only be requiring to take it out once, perhaps twice, a year. He couldn't resist showing the object of his delight to the bank manager, Mr Sedgley.

'You'll be wearing it for Mayor-making day, no doubt?' Mr Sedgley enquired.

'If I'm invited,' said Gerald.

'Oh, I feel sure Ramsbottom will want all his old friends to witness the ceremony. Especially you, I suspect,' he added without explanation.

⋆ ⋆ ⋆

Gerald read the news item in the Court Circular of *The Times* to his wife over breakfast: 'It has been announced from Buckingham Palace that King Alfons IV of Multavia will make a state visit to Britain between April 7th and 11th.'

'I wonder if we will have an opportunity to meet the King again,' said Angela.

Gerald offered no opinion.

In fact Mr and Mrs Gerald Haskins received two invitations connected with King Alfons's official visit, one to dine with the King at Claridge's — Multavia's London Embassy not being large enough to cater for such an occasion — and the second arriving a day later by special delivery from Buckingham Palace.

Gerald was delighted. The Peacock, it seemed, was going to get three outings in one month, as their visit to the Palace was ten days before Walter Ramsbottom would be installed as Mayor.

The state dinner at Claridge's was memorable, and although there were several hundred other guests Gerald still managed to catch a moment with his host, King Alfons IV, who, he found to his pleasure, could not take his eyes off the Order of the Peacock (Third Class).

The trip to Buckingham Palace a week later was Gerald and Angela's second, following Gerald's investiture in 1984 as a Commander of the British Empire. It took Gerald almost as long to dress for the state occasion as it did his wife. He took some time fiddling with his collar to be sure that his CBE could be seen to its full advantage while the Order of the Peacock still rested squarely on his shoulders. Gerald had asked his tailor to sew little loops into his tailcoat so that the Order did not have to be continually readjusted.

When the Haskins arrived at Buckingham Palace they followed a throng of bemedalled men and tiara'd ladies through to the state dining room, where a footman handed out seating cards to each of the guests. Gerald unfolded his to find an arrow pointing to his name. he took his wife by the arm and guided her to their places.

He noticed that Angela's head kept turning whenever she saw a tiara.

Although they were seated some distance away from Her Majesty at an offshoot of the main table, there was still a minor royal on Gerald's left and the Minister of Agriculture on his right. He was more than satisfied. In fact the whole evening went far too quickly, and Gerald was already beginning to feel that Mayor-making day would be something of an anti-climax. Nevertheless, Gerald imagined a scene where Councillor Ramsbottom was admiring the Order of the Peacock (Third Class) while he was telling him about the dinner at the Palace.

After two loyal toasts and two national anthems the Queen rose to her feet. She spoke warmly of Multavia as she addressed her three hundred guests, and affectionately of her distant cousin the King. Her Majesty added that she hoped to visit his kingdom at some time in the near future. This was greeted with considerable applause. She then concluded her speech by saying it was her intention to make two investitures.

The Queen created King Alfons IV a Knight Commander of the Royal Victorian Order (KCVO), and then Multavia's Ambassador to the Court of St James a Commander of the same order (CVO), both being personal orders of the monarch. A box of royal blue was opened by the Court Chamberlain and the awards placed over the recipients' shoulders. As soon as the Queen had completed her formal duties, King Alfons rose to make his reply.

'Your Majesty,' he continued after the usual formalities and thanks had been completed, 'I also would like to make two awards. The first is to an Englishman who has given great service to my country through his expertise and diligence'

— the King glanced in Gerald's direction. 'A man,' he continued, 'who completed a feat of sanitary engineering that any nation on earth could be proud of and indeed, Your Majesty, it was opened by your own Foreign Secretary. We in the capital of Teske will remain in his debt for generations to come. We therefore bestow on Mr Gerald Haskins, CBE, the Order of the Peacock (Second Class).'

Gerald couldn't believe his ears.

Tumultuous applause greeted a surprised Gerald as he made his way up towards their Majesties. He came to a standstill behind the gilt chairs somewhere between the Queen of England and the King of Multavia. The King smiled at the new recipient of the Order of the Peacock (Second Class) as the two men shook hands. But before bestowing the new honour upon him, King Alfons leaned forward and with some difficulty removed from Gerald's shoulders his Order of the Peacock (Third Class).

'You won't be needing this any longer,' the King whispered in Gerald's ear.

Gerald watched in horror as his prize possession disappeared into a red leather box held open by the King's private secretary, who stood poised behind his sovereign. Gerald continued to stare at the private secretary, who was either a diplomat of the highest order or had not been privy to the King's plan, for his face showed no sign of anything untoward. Once Gerald's magnificent prize had been safely removed, the box snapped closed like a safe of which Gerald had not been told the combination.

Gerald wanted to protest, but remained speechless.

King Alfons then removed from another box the Order of the Peacock (Second Class) and placed it over Gerald's shoulders. Gerald, staring at the indifferent coloured glass stones, hesitated for a few moments before stumbling a pace back, bowing, and then returning to his place in the great dining room. He did not hear the waves of applause that accompanied him; his only thought was how he could possibly retrieve his lost chain immediately the speeches were over. He slumped down in the chair next to his wife.

'And now,' continued the King, 'I wish to present a decoration that has not been bestowed on anyone since my late father's death. The Order of the Peacock (First Class), which it gives me special delight to bestow on Her Majesty Queen Elizabeth II.'

The Queen rose from her place as the King's private secretary once again stepped forward. In his hands was the same red leather case that had snapped shut so firmly on Gerald's unique possession. The case was reopened and the King removed the magnificent Order from the box and placed it on the shoulders of the Queen. The jewels sparkled in the candlelight, and the guests gasped at the sheer magnificence of the piece.

Gerald was the only person in the room who knew its true value.

'Well, you always said it was fit for a monarch,'

his wife remarked as she touched her string of pearls.

'Aye,' said Gerald. 'But what's Ramsbottom going to say when he sees this?' he added sadly, fingering the Order of the Peacock (Second Class). 'He'll know it's not the real thing.'

'I don't see it matters that much,' said Angela.

'What do you mean, lass?' asked Gerald. 'I'll be the laughing stock of Hull on Mayor-making day.'

'You should start reading the evening papers, Gerald, and stop looking in mirrors, and then you'd know Walter isn't going to be Mayor this year.'

'Not going to be Mayor?' repeated Gerald.

'No. The present Mayor has opted to do a second term, so Walter won't be Mayor until next year.'

'Is that right?' said Gerald with a smile.

'And if you're thinking what I think you're thinking, Gerald Haskins, this time it's going to cost you a tiara.'

Other titles in the
Charnwood Library Series:

LOVE ME OR LEAVE ME

Josephine Cox

Beautiful Eva Bereton has only three friends in the world: Patsy, who she looks upon as a sister; Bill, her adopted cousin, and her mother, to whom she is devoted. With Eva's father increasingly angry about life as a cripple, she and her mother support each other, keeping their spirits high despite the abuse. So when a tragic accident robs Eva of both parents, Patsy, a loveable Irish rogue, is the only one left to support her. Tragedy strikes yet again when Eva's uncle comes to reclaim the farm that Eva had always believed belonged to her parents. Together with Patsy, Eva has no choice but to start a new life far away . . .

THE DEATH ZONE

Matt Dickinson

Ten expeditions were high on Everest, preparing for their summit push. They set out in perfect conditions on 10 May 1996. But twenty-four hours later, eight climbers were dead and a further three were to die, victims of one of the most devastating storms ever to hit the mountain. On the North Face, a British expedition found itself in the thick of the drama. Against all the odds, film-maker Matt Dickinson and professional climber Alan Hinkes managed to battle through hurricane-force winds to reach the summit. This is Matt Dickinson's extraordinary story of human triumph, folly and disaster.

STILL WATER

John Harvey

The naked body of a young woman is found floating in an inner-city canal. Not the first, nor the last. When another woman disappears, following a seminar on women and violence, everyone fears for her safety — especially those who know about her husband's controlling character. Is this a one-off domestic crime or part of a wider series of murders? What else has been simmering beneath this couple's apparently normal middle-class life? As Resnick explores deeper, he finds disturbing parallels between the couple he's investigating and his own evolving relationship with Hannah Campbell.

AN APRIL SHROUD

Reginald Hill

After seeing Inspector Pascoe off on his honeymoon, Superintendent Andy Dalziel runs into trouble on his own holiday. He accompanies his rescuers back to their rundown mansion, where he discovers that Lake House's owner, Bonnie Fielding, seems less troubled by her husband's tragic death than by the problem of completing the Banqueting Hall. Prompted not only by a professional curiosity — why would anyone want to keep a dead rat in a freezer? — but also by Mrs Fielding's ample charms, Dalziel stays on. By the time Pascoe reappears, there have been several more deaths . . .

TREVOR McDONALD FAVOURITE POEMS

Trevor McDonald

Trevor McDonald, popular newscaster and also Chairman of the Campaign for Better Use of the English Language, has now compiled an anthology of his favourite poetry from across the ages. The collection is based on material published in his regular Anthology column in the *Daily Telegraph*. It is a comprehensive introduction to the poetry of the English language, from Milton to Ted Hughes, from Britain and abroad. He has included both perennial favourites and less familiar but accessible poetry. Each poet is introduced with a concise history of their work and there is something to suit all tastes and moods.